A SECOND CHANCE VOLUME 2
BY EDMOND WHITE

Table of Contents

TABLE OF CONTENTS

DAVID

18

Ray's Café, Montreal, Canada

"David, you've had enough. Save some for next time."

"Don't tell me I had enough," David snaps. "I can drink as much as I want. I'm not driving, remember? You are."

"It doesn't matter. You're destroying yourself. It's the third night in a row. I'm not going to sit here and allow you to kill yourself. You're in good health, David, but at the rate you're going, you will end up dead."

"That doesn't sound so bad at all. You see, death and I have a love-take relationship. Everything I loved in my life, death, has taken it from me. If death wants me, he can have me. I'm ready to meet him, mono y mono."

"David, that's crazy talk. Why would you want to die?"

"What do I have to live for? Everything that has meant something to me is gone. The one thing I always depended on in times of trouble is gone. I can't even play football anymore. I'm not good at anything else," he hangs his head.

"David, one day, you can return to the field. The doctor said your condition can change at a moment's notice."

"How Cedric? I'm blind. Did you forget that already?"

"I know you're blind, but not permanently. You suffered a concussion, that's it. Your sight may return."

"It's been a month. I can't see anything but darkness. Do you know what it's like not to be able to see? I don't even remember how I looked or what I look like now. I used to watch the sunset and the bright moonlit night. My sight is never coming back," David puts the empty glass to his mouth.

"I've been praying for you every day. Samantha and I attend a small Baptist church on Sundays and Wednesdays. They have a session called the sweet hour of prayer. Anyone in the congregation can come to the church altar and pray. I spend much of my time pouring my heart out to God, asking him to cure you."

"Sorry to bust your bubble, but God doesn't exist. I guess your praying was all for nothing. When we die, and that's it. No heaven, nor hell, just death," Cedric disagrees with his justification. He feels sad for David.

"How can you say this?"

"How can I say this? Take a close look at my life. If there is a God, why did he let my parents die in front of me? I was only a baby Cedric. He let my grandmother die, and Uncle Chuck is on his deathbed with lung cancer."

"Unfortunately, they died, but you lived. God allowed you to play football at a higher level than most. You have a gift many would kill for."

"You call a blind running back a gift? How can I play now? And as far as my talent is concerned, I taught myself. God has nothing to do with my ability," Cedric cringes inside. He is fearful of David's lack of faith.

"David, please listen to me. I think God wants more from you. He made you fearless and strong to face difficulty. God had to get your attention. I think he's speaking to you," David slams his empty glass against the bar, getting Ray's attention.

"If he's talking to me, why can't I hear him?"

"You have to search for him, and then you will hear him," David laughs.

"There's no God, Cedric, only life and death. You know what I hear, Cedric? I hear everything. When I lost my sight, it made my other senses stronger. I guess I'm more in tune with them. My hearing picks up noises from a distance. Like right now, I hear the men sitting behind me. They've been talking about me since we've sat down. They say I deserve this because I think I'm better than the team. Everyone in here seems to have an opinion about me. The two women at the end of the bar are also talking about me. One is telling the other she feels awful for my plight."

"David, you can hear all of this?" Cedric sounds surprised.

"Yeah, when I focus or when I'm not drunk. My sense of smell has improved as well. I can smell every scent in this bar. From your cheap cologne to the Beyoncé perfume the woman at the end of the bar is wearing."

"David, that's something else. You lost one sense but have gained more strength in the others."

"What's so special about it? You know the one thing I can't hear or smell?"

"What?"

"God, because he doesn't exist."

"Ask, seek, and knock."

"What's that, a title from a book?" Cedric's patience is beginning to wear thin.

"No, David, it's scripture. Ask, and he will be answered. Seek, and he will find. Knock, and the doors shall be open. You only have to believe in him, and he will save you."

"I don't believe in him, so I assume he will never answer me. Faith is such a waste, Cedric," David detests. "When have you become so holy, Mr. Married man that likes to stare at other women?"

"I'm not holy but only human and born to make mistakes with God helping me to correct them along the way." David is getting tired of hearing Cedric preach about a God that isn't real. He needs more beer to help him forget about everything, specifically this stupid conversation.

"Ray, can I please have another drink?"

"I have to agree with Cedric. No more drinks. You're over your limit."

"Ray, it's me, David. I've been patronizing this café since I arrived in Montreal. Just one more. I need one more drink."

"David, you know I run a tight ship around here. You've seen me stop others from drinking their lives away." Ray Turner followed David's college career and was thrilled when he decided to leave the States for Canada. When David first walked into his café two years ago, Ray made him feel like a Canadian. Their relationship blossomed into something special from the very beginning. Ray is a knowledgeable sports fan. He loves to talk about any sport, and so does David. To watch David in this condition hurts Ray enormously. David was on top of the world—a genuine scoring machine and then regulated to a bar stool without warning. Resembling Pat Riley, Ray slides his fingers through his slick salt and peppered hair and decides to give David a glass of water instead.

"Here, David, this is your last drink," Ray nods reassuringly at Cedric.

"I knew you would give in. Thanks a bunch," David feels for the glass. He turns up the glass as water trickles down his throat. "

"Water? He slams down the glass. Come on, Ray, don't do this to me. I deserve better."

"You deserve to live. I refuse to be the reason for your demise. Cedric, bring him home at once."

"I'm way past twelve, Ray. I take orders from no one. You and Cedric can't tell me what to do. I'll leave when I'm good and ready to leave," David tries to maneuver himself off the bar stool and falls onto the floor. A chorus of laughs erupts, angering him. Cedric rushes to his aide.

"Get away from me. I can get up on my own. I don't need your pity. I'm fine," David yells. Cedric and Ray watch in agony as David tries to crawl back to the bar stool. The laughter stops when the patrons realize he is blind. David turns around to face where the laughter came from. He carefully gets to his feet, holding onto the bar stool for support.

"I'm glad I'm your circus show. I may have lost my sight, but I can hear all of you. Some of you think I only care about myself. That is far from the truth. And some of you pity me. I don't need anyone feeling sorry for me. I can handle it. I'm used to adversity. Isn't that right, God?"

PAUL

19

Family Day is taking place at Bedford Mental Institution. Usually, one visitor at a time can visit a patient with proper approval. On this particular day, the institution decides to permit four members from the immediate family. The sign above the door reads "family matters" in white, blue, and red interchangeable letters. Big smiles and laughter serenade the room. This occasion is a joyous time for many of the patients. With sheer excitement, the patients enthusiastically hold onto every word their loved ones share concerning news back home. I have to admit everyone seems happy, even uptight Harold. His granddaughter bounces around the room as her small arsenal of braids encased in white beads dangles in the air. Her small, golden-brown face glows. She stops bouncing momentarily and reaches inside her white CVS bag, pulling out a blue envelope. She hands it to Harold. Harold's large hands slowly pry open the envelope, gaining access to a shiny get well soon card. Harold recites the card aloud, adoring its content. He then lifts his granddaughter over his head and thanks her while smiling ear to ear. A variety of delicious foods and tasty desserts line the tables.

The mouthwatering aroma makes it hard to resist. I made a plate of baked macaroni and cheese, barbeque chicken, mashed potatoes with gravy, and a small slice of cheesecake for myself. Family members reminisce about happier times as I eat alone at my table. The family members make their special someone feel human again by allocating essential dates and periods in which significant events transpired. Even Bryson revels in the festivities. His best friend from high school, a slim, skinny kid with acne, has come to show him support, as well as his mother and father. Bryson is thrilled. He cannot stop asking questions. The food is delicious. I contemplate getting seconds, but my stomach persuades me otherwise. I walk to the trash can to throw away my plate when Alex approaches.

"Hi Paul, I want to introduce you to my family."

"Okay, where are they?"

"The extra table to the far right," she points.

"Ok, I see them now."

Alex doesn't look like her regular defeated self. Alexandria is definitely in the building. The black strapless dress she's wearing accentuates her full-bodied figure. She triggers a response, causing women to pull their husbands in tighter. Her cover girl exterior and long jet-black hair make everyone take notice. I even find myself in awe of her natural beauty.

"Paul, this is my mother, father, and only brother Danny."

"Hi Paul, I'm Olivia," her mother says in a strong Italian accent, reaching to shake my hand. Alexandria undeniably acquired her looks from her mom. Olivia has the same dark, mysterious eyes as Alexandria. She has a gray and black plaid dress, black leather boots, silver earrings, and a fur coat. A touch of red lipstick enhances her middle-aged features, making Olivia appear as young as Alexandria.

"Well, Alexandria, now I know where your look comes from. You two can almost pass as twins, But I think mom is prettier," Olivia blushes, thanking me. The skin tenor of her mother and father are perfectly tanned as if they spend every wakening summer taking in the sun.

"Alexandria has told us so much about you. She talks about you quite often. Thanks for making her feel at home. Since her stay here, she hasn't been able to connect with any of the others. I think you have helped her to feel better about herself. She's been through so much."

"Alexandria has helped me also. Reaching out to her daily has strengthened my perspective on life. This place gets to you after a while. When I talk with Alexandria, I find myself being a pastor again and having a sense of purpose."

"Hi Paul, I'm Vincent," her father interrupts firmly, shaking my hand. "And this is my son Danny," Danny nods, acknowledging me, then turns his head. He seems angry and withdrawn. Danny is somewhat taller than his dad with a few pimples, wearing blue skinny jeans and a New York Knicks jacket. He doesn't have Alexandria's dark, mysterious eyes, but he has jet-black hair. His eyes are more like his father's, a smoked gray. Her father is small, slender, well groomed, and dressed in all maroon, with a stylish gold chain. Alexandria's brother is detached from our conversation. His lack of interest annoys Olivia.

"Danny, my dear, aren't you going to introduce yourself?"

"For what, Mom? Is it important?" He raises his voice. "He's a friend of Alex, not a friend of mine. My friends are enjoying the basketball game you wouldn't let me attend. You and Dad made me come to this nut house. It's always about Alex and never about me. Why must I sit through this? She will never get better. They're all just crazy psychopaths, and Alex is crazier than everybody in here. Danny's outburst distracts the other families. Everyone stares at Alexandria, awaiting her reaction. Turning red from embarrassment and shame, Alexandria looks around the room and darts off crying. Olivia follows after her.

"Are you satisfied, Danny? Your sister needs our support right now. What kind of brother are you to talk to her like this? What has she ever done to you? Take my keys and go to the car. Get out of my sight!" Danny walks away without saying a word.

"I'm sorry, Paul. My son is young, and he doesn't fully understand. Olivia and I had Danny very late. They're fifteen years apart. When Alexandria developed a mental illness, we spent most of our time tending to her needs. In the process, we unintentionally neglected Danny. He is now seventeen and very rebellious, as you can see," her father shows very little emotion, but I can see the disguised pain in his eyes.

"I understand, Mr. Perotti, there's no need for an apology. How did Alexandria get to this point in her life?"

"A terrible man led her astray."

"A boyfriend?"

"If that's what you want to call him. His name should be Satan. After meeting Andy, everything positive in her life changed. Before meeting him, she had her apartment, a nice car, and a great job as a drug and alcohol counselor. Alex loves helping people rid themselves of their dependencies. She put in long hours even when overtime funding wasn't available."

"Wow, a counselor. I would've never guessed it."

"Yes, and a very good one," he begins to let his feelings emerge, showing more emotion.

"Alexandria met Andy at the clinic where she worked. He was one of her clients. She didn't believe in involving her clients; it was also against policy. Andy was a persistent bastard."

"As a pastor, I face the same situations as Alexandria. Maintaining professionalism can be problematic when your clients refuse to listen."

"One day, Olivia and I decided to visit Alexandria's apartment. You know, a surprise visit. My wife had cooked her favorite lasagna dish. So we decided to bring her some. When I ring the bell, this ingrate only opens her door in boxers."

"Boxers, that's it?" I ask, thinking he could have been completely naked. How fortunate for him and Olivia.

"That's it, like he owned the place. And you know something else? He asks, enraged.

"What?"

"La brutta parola! I look at Vincent, waiting for him to translate. He looks back at me with a sickening expression. It means ugly. The son of a bitch is ugly. He reminds me of a scraggly pet Alexandria once had when she was just a child." I then start wondering, what if he's black? Some people get a kick out of comparing black people to animals. Deep down inside, I was afraid to ask, but I must find out. There's no way I will stand here and allow him to insult my race. It doesn't matter if he's Alexandria's father or not.

"Vincent, what does he look like?" I ask with uneasy anticipation.

"Pale white and skinny, anorexic, like the life has been sucked out of him. You can see his cheekbones, for Christ's sake! His hair is unkempt, and he has dark circles around the eyes." *What a relief, I thought.*

"Her apartment was filthy. Dirty dishes piled up in the sink, roaches crawling everywhere, smelly garbage and clothes everywhere. Her boyfriend even had the nerve to have a picture of his fat, ugly mother hanging on her living room wall. My wife and I couldn't believe it. Alexandria has always been a tidy person. She hates clutter and filth. I think she felt sorry for the bastard. Alexandria has a soft spot. That's one of her biggest problems. She cares too much for others and not enough for herself."

"Caring is a good thing, Vincent. Your daughter has compassion for the weak and less fortunate. I am also guilty of this."

"I think caring is fine, but to a certain extent. You can only help those who want help. If people are bringing you down with them, then they must go," what Vincent said makes a lot of sense.

"Vincent, I agree. There are so many poor and homeless individuals with numerous addictions who refuse to better themselves. Even when helped, they continue to remain the same. Sometimes, we must know when to let them go, or we will fall along with them."

"Alexandria told us she loved him, and they were getting married. My wife almost passed out. I wanted to kill him right there in her apartment. As months passed, she spent more time with his family and less and less time with us. He manipulated her. His family said she wasn't pretty. His mother dared to say my daughter is ugly. Can you believe this? This fat ugly cow is calling my Alexandria ugly? Alexandria fell for it. She started dressing more like a man than a woman. She neglected her home, family, and her life. He persuaded her to try heroin. Ever since then, her addiction has gotten worse."

"Alexandria is a beautiful woman. It sounds to me like he felt insecure around her. Andy probably couldn't believe she would choose him. So, to ease his insecurities, he degrades her, which makes him feel equal. He's played a vicious mental game on Alexandria."

"Paul, I think suicide was her escape. She dislikes what she has become and has lost everything in the process. That's my daughter in there. I want the best for her. My daughter is very fond of you; you're a swell person. I know what happened to you on the outside. But remember one thing: when we fall, we get back up. It's easy to lie down and give up, but overcoming our fears and failures takes strength. So, when you get back up, Paul and I know you will take Alexandria with you. See you soon. Take care of yourself."

I dwell on Alexandria after he walks out and imagine the two of us together with many of the same characteristics. We have three things in common: attempted suicide, counseling, and a good heart. I'm unsure if these features can keep a relationship intact, especially the first one. If Vincent is giving his approval, then I might as well try. I like Alexandria a lot, and I know she feels the same. I visualize her helping me with the church. As a drug and alcohol counselor, she's qualified to save people in the community with their addictions. My church is large enough to have a class designed to accomplish this mission. I'm sure she would agree and love the idea.

"Paul?" Her voice startles me. I turn to see my sister standing in the doorway. After five long months, she finally decides to appear. I can't imagine why. When I needed her the most, she abandoned me. I have a ton of emotions brewing inside. I feel rage, anger, and mistrust. I also think of adoration, retrieval, and gratitude. I don't know whether to yell at her or to give her a big hug. My attempt to fight back the tears fails miserably. She stands there frozen, not knowing what to say. An uncomfortable minute passes without a word from either of us. I elect to break the ice by walking over and hugging her for what seems like an eternity.

"Paul," she calls out my name and wipes her face. "I'm sorry for not being there for you. I just got caught up in all the mayhem. The church has slandered your name to the lowermost level. Your so-called friends have turned against you. Even Mama refuses to say your name. WTUV news aired a special a few weeks ago. It was called "A Pastor's Fall from Grace". Danita Stokes ran the story. She will denigrate her mother if it means getting ratings. I'm sure everyone has seen it, aired over and over." *It feels good to hear Sheila's voice, the comforting voice of reason that saved me in the past when my father died. She will tell me everything I need to know; even if it's not what I want to hear.*

"How have you been?"

"I'm surviving. The facility treats me fairly well, but I miss the outside. I miss preaching, I miss the sounds of the city, I miss home, and I miss Mom. They have turned against me, but I'm ready to clear my name."

"It's not going to be that easy, Paul. You don't seem to understand. Patricia has done a masterful job slandering your name. Your fingerprints are all over the apartment. There are so many pictures of you two together and letters."

"Letters? What kind of letters? I only wrote her once, saying I missed her," she looked at me awkwardly before answering.

"The police found twenty letters."

"Twenty letters concerning what? Did the police check the handwriting? I wrote to her in black ink. I never typed anything."

"The letters had black ink with the same penmanship as yours."

"What did the letters say?"

"The police wouldn't let me see the letters. It's still under investigation. I think they have enough evidence to convict you."

"Convict me of what?"

"Patricia looked badly beaten, and your DNA is all over her apartment. There were pictures and letters, and you had unprotected sex with her. And to top it all off, you tried to kill yourself, which makes you guilty."

"Shelia, I'm in love with her."

"You need to snap out of it. I know you haven't had any in a very long time, but it's probably the sex that has your thinking distorted."

"It's more than sex. Patricia is always on my mind. I can't seem to shake her."

"Did you tell the doctor the same thing you're telling me?"

"Somewhat."

"Then how are you supposed to get better?"

"I can't tell him."

"Why?"

"I feel ashamed."

"For falling in love with a woman? Are you kidding me, Paul?"

"I'm a pastor, Sheila. I let her deceive me. I've fallen so far."

"How many times did you sleep with her?"

"That's what I mean; I only slept with her once. I may have wanted her many other times. I desired her, but I controlled my emotions up to that point. I told her we must wait for marriage and do things correctly. I allowed myself to be put in a situation to see her naked. I was unable to resist. She has control over me. When she isn't around, I think of nothing but her. She's become my entire focus. My sermons in the church started to suffer. I stopped praying to God, and my level of positive thinking has become negative. It's part of the reason why I'm here. She even asked me if I would stop preaching after she made love to me."

"What did you say?"

"I told her I would think about it."

"She pussy whipped you after one time? How in the world can you be this strung out?"

"I don't know, Shelia. I even have dreams about her."

"Man, you have it bad. So what's your prognosis?"

"The doctor says I'm getting there, one step at a time."

"You must take larger steps because we have so much work. We need to find out the reason why Patricia is trying to destroy your life and clear your name."

"Amen, I agree. Why is all of this happening to me?"

"Let me ask you something else, Paul. Did you think your life would be different just because you're a pastor? Temptation comes to all of us, especially those who are serving God," she folds her arms, giving me a staid look.

"Not really, but I know I'm doing God's work, and he will recognize it. Therefore, he will protect me."

"Satan can also recognize it and cause a lot of confusion. Stepping into the pulpit is hard work, as you know. I remember how Daddy struggled. Satan comes after us in many forms when we least expect it. It's easy to see someone else's shortcomings but not our own."

"Sheila, you're talking to a minister. I know this already."

"It seems to me that you have forgotten." *Sheila resembles my mother and sometimes acts like her. She is ten years older than me. I inherited the lighter complexion from my dad, and she acquired the darker skin tone from my mother. People don't realize our relationship because of our different skin textures. Shelia has my mother's sun-brown eyes and thick body. The women on my mother's side of the family have protruding hips and thighs that most men worship. We do have the same wide nose and round cheeks.*

"Remember, brother, we come from a family of preachers. I do know what I'm talking about. You might have gone to divinity school receiving your college degree, but don't forget who helped you along the way."

"I can't ever forget. You've done so much for me."

"OK, no more mushy talk. Get better so you can leave with me soon. I will visit you more often until you're released. I promise. What days am I allowed to visit?"

"Visiting hours are between twelve and four on Monday through Sunday. The only day you cannot visit is the second Wednesday of each month. There is a monthly mandatory safety drill," we smile, embracing each other again."

"Yes."

"Hurry up and get well. I'll see you later."

"Ok, bye."

Club Silhouettes New Haven, CT.

The syncopation of hard-hitting beats blaring through speakers intending to make you move. It's Friday afternoon happy hour, and Silhouettes is jumping as usual. Practically, everyone is having a great time. The electric atmosphere makes for a perfect celebration. Downing shot glasses and beer bottles are the norm, allowing everyone to get their drink on. It's not a large club, but Silhouettes is big enough to hold a small number of people, the size of a hundred, who need a break from their daily routines. A couple of women dancing in the center of the floor attract attention from onlookers. The two women are grinding each other in skimpy clothing while the small crowd of lesbians joins in. A blue and white strobe light orbits the dance floor, creating a slow-motion illusion.

"Francine, what's wrong with you tonight? You're not your normal self," Maria yells over the music.

"I'm ok."

"Louder Francine, I can't hear you."

"I said I'm ok. Can you hear me now?" She shouts.

"Francine, I know when something's bothering you. We've been seeing each other for three years, and I know you all too well."

"Is that a fact, Maria?" Francine cracks a smile.

"Girl, you know it is. I love you to death. So what's wrong, baby girl?"

"I'm just a little stressed from work. It's nothing major."

"How many times have I told you to leave that place? You need to find something you went to school for."

"I know, but it's decent pay, and the benefits are great."

"How can you work around those psycho's anyway? I couldn't. I would be too afraid of one of them hurting me. Do you ever feel scared around them?"

"Sometimes, but the staff does a great job protecting us."

"Well, leave work at work, and let's have some fun," Maria says, preparing for another shot of dry Vodka.

"Your right, let's have fun, but first another shot," the two women both suck down on lemons before tilting their heads back to swallow the strong vodka. Maria slams her shot glass on the table, and Francine follows suit. Maria Sanchez is wearing a tight pink mini skirt, black fishnet stockings, and a pink blouse unbuttoned at the top. She has an incredible figure with strong Mexican genes and a great attitude. Francine loves Maria. Maria makes her feel like a true woman. She met Maria when her boyfriend cheated on her. He found pleasure in sleeping with whoever and whenever he wanted, even Francine's best friend. Francine was devastated and gave up on men altogether. She started frequenting gay clubs to see if women were any different. Surprisingly, she found someone not only other, but Maria gave her self-assurance.

"Francine, I'm going to the lady's room. When I return, we'll dance the night away."

"I'm looking forward to it. I'll be here waiting for you," Maria walks off tipsy, stumbling on her way to the ladies' room. How can she tell Maria she's seeing someone else, someone more beautiful, intriguing, desirable, and perfect? Guilt consumes her heart. Maria has been there for her, rebuilding the backbone her ex-boyfriend destroyed. Her feelings are so vital for Maria. However, Francine's new love interest commands her complete attention. Her latest love interest is at the bar near Francine's table. Francine is unaware of her presence.

"Girl, are you ready to dance?" Maria asks, returning from the bathroom.

"I sure am. Let's do this," Maria grabs Francine by the hand, leading her to the small square dance floor. Francine watches her Mexican girlfriend move with absolute grace. Her feet strut in a flawless rhythm as her hips sway back and forth. She grabs Maria closer as the two of them dance at pace together. The dance floor is hot and crowded. Francine holds onto Maria tightly. She closes her eyes and pretends Maria is her new love interest. She spins Maria around. In the process, Maria loses her balance. Francine quickly extends her arms, pulling Maria back in. She saves her from embarrassment. Maria laughs at her minor debacle, continuing in stride. Francine once again closes her eyes, allowing the music to take over. The club's temperature is rising. She removes her blue blazer, letting it drop to the floor. Suddenly, an excited dancer accidentally bumps Francine, irritating her. Her fantasy and terrific mood are temporarily lost. She doesn't get upset and realizes the dance floor is overcrowded. It's probably accidental. Francine clears her thoughts once again, letting the music do its purpose. Electronic dance music becomes faster, producing a heightened response from its dance participants. The thumping techno beats accelerate.

Everyone is now jumping up and down, clapping their hands. Another forceful push against Francine's back is the final straw. Angrily, she turns around, preparing herself for a fight. Francine had once broken a woman's nose for touching Maria's hair. Growing up in a household of five boys and being the only girl, she learned to protect herself. She fought constantly with her brothers, even delivering the eldest brother a black eye. Francine stands a tiny five feet two and weighs one hundred twenty pounds. The size of her opposition doesn't matter. She fully understands the art of war. She whirls around on her heels.

"That's the last time," she yells before realizing who pushes her. Her new love interest stands before her. She wants her right at this moment. Her new friend takes her hand, places a napkin in her palm, and then quickly moves away.

"Girl, are you alright?"

"I'm fine, Maria. It was just an accident."

"So, did she apologize?"

"You know she did."

"I know how you get. Don't start a fight in here. I want to dance tonight."

"Maria, I'm thirsty. Can you please get me a drink?"

"What do you want?"

"Another shot of Ciroc."

"The line is pretty long. It might take forever."

"I'll wait for you at the table."

Francine observes and keeps a close eye on Maria. In haste, she opens the brown napkin. Her heart skips as she reads "Meet Me in the Ladies Room," written in red lipstick—a prominent smile forms across her face. Francine walks over to a frustrated Maria standing in line.

"I'm going to the lady's room."

"Well, I'll be right here in this awful long line. Don't kill the fish," she says, laughing, getting half a smile from Francine as she rushes off.

Francine's palms sweat with nervous anticipation from the possibility of Maria catching her. She hadn't seen her friend in two weeks but was delighted to find her here. When Francine stepped inside the bathroom, she noticed three other women. There is no sign of her friend. All three women are busy doing something different. A tall white woman dressed in a catsuit is preparing her makeup. Next to her, a dark Hispanic female straightens her blond wig. And next to her, a short black woman at the end is fixing her panties. There are four stalls in the perfume-scented bathroom.

Francine inconspicuously checks each booth. The first stall is empty except for a bunch of loaded tampons. The Second and third stalls are empty as well. Francine hesitates before opening the fourth stall. Disappointment begins to sink in. She doesn't want to open the stall door, not finding her friend inside. It's been too long since she last held her and felt the warmth of her body. She craves her irresistible scent and the satisfying taste of her tongue. Whenever she appears, it's always by surprise. The three women exit the bathroom one by one, leaving Francine alone. Francine hears her own heart pulsating from the accelerated rush of adrenaline. She pushes the door open, discovering her new love interest standing bare naked over the toilet seat. Her stunning sculptured frame sends chills through Francine. She clutches Francine's hair, pulling her in to taste her heat.

CHINA

20

Buckland, Pennsylvania County, is near the Ohio state line. The area resembles an old Mid-Western town containing green pastures and overstretched hills. Many of the homes are relatively close to each other, leaving little space for privacy among their neighbors. Mark doesn't have a green thumb but spends much time tending to his lawn. He keeps the hedges trimmed and waters his plants aligned around his front porch in the summer. If he had any drawbacks about Pennsylvania, it has to do with the snow. Vast snowfall during the winter months makes commuting to work difficult. Snow blowers and shovels are a necessity if you live in Buckland County. It is no comparison to the farm his parents had to sell due to the lack of hands to maintain it, but his ranch-style single-family home is more than enough. He doesn't mind the closeness of each neighbor, considering his parents live to his right and his aunt Shirley on the left.

When the house went on the market, he wasted no time purchasing it to stay close to his family. After shoveling the snow out of his driveway, Mark leans over the front porch to catch his breath.

"Mark?" His mother calls from her doorway, bundled up to stay warm.

"Yes, mam?" Mark answers his mother like he did as a child, with the highest respect.

"Would you like a cup of hot chocolate? I know you must be freezing."

"Yes, I can use some. I'm tired of seeing snow," Mark rubs his hands together.

His mother is using a broom to sweep snow away from her porch. Her facial features haven't changed since Mark was a child. His mother is sixty-five years old but can pass for fifty on any given day. Her dark skin is clear of wrinkles, and her brown eyes are full of wisdom. She stops sweeping for a moment to adjust her hat and scarf. She then continues.

"Mam, do you want me to sweep that for you?" He asks, standing on the first two steps of her porch.

"No, it's good exercise for me. Your hot chocolate is over there on the ledge."

"After I finish this hot chocolate, I will shovel the driveway for you. I don't mind; I know Dad can't get around like he used to."

"You're a good son, Mark. More than I can say about those two brothers of yours," she says, never taking her eyes off the task.

"The two of them have different ways. Their good men, though."

"If you say so, Mark, I haven't heard from Benny or Gerald in weeks. They both know your father isn't doing too well, so they can at least call. Is that too hard to do?"

"No, not at all. I will call Benny and Gerald," his mother elects to redirect the conversation.

"Mark, guess who called me today?"

"Who, mam?"

"Kelly." *Mark knew she would try to contact his mother after he ignored her calls. He doesn't want anything to do with Kelly or China. As far as he's concerned, that life is behind him.*

"What did she want?" He asks with an absolute lack of interest. His mother stops sweeping and lifts her head. She frowns at Mark before responding.

"I raised you better than this. Your father and I taught you how to be a man. A respectful man, a God-fearing man, a man who knows the difference between right and wrong, and a man who can swallow his pride and know how to forgive. Mark, that woman loves you. Can't you see that? China's disabled, for heaven's sake! How can you sit here and not wonder how she's doing? Her life is a mess. She needs you in her life more than ever before. Kelly says her home is a disaster. She refuses to answer any of her calls, and this week, she cut ties with Kelly as her manager. She needs help. I know your heart still beats for her. Go over there and help her, at least. Will you please?" Mark takes a moment to respond, taking it all in.

"Mam, you know I will do anything for China, but it hurt when she chose her fans over me—five years of my life wasted. I want a family. I'm not getting any younger. What I want doesn't seem to matter to her."

"She's a celebrity, son. Her shoes are much bigger to fill than yours. How do you think she got where she is today? Her fans made her a star, and she's repaying them for what they've done for her."

"Hasn't she repaid them enough already? She's put her happiness on hold, our happiness. Do you listen to the news or read the paper, mam?"

"I refuse to read that garbage, particularly the Buckland Tribune. Everything in there is lies and propaganda."

"Some of it's real, like last week's article about China. The article said she has lost a lot of her fan base. People are not buying her music as much as they were before her accident. She's dedicated her life to these people, and this is how they repay her. The paper even called her a thing of the past."

"Mark, doesn't that bother you?"

"Not really."

"Why not?"

"China made her bed," his mother turns irate. She lets the broom fall on the porch.

"She's made her bed? Is that all you can say about the woman you want to marry? It seems to me you never really loved her. How could you say that?"

"Mam, I love her. I love her more than anything on this earth. She doesn't deserve my love. She abused it."

"Let me share something with you, Mr. high and mighty. You need to hold onto something good when it comes into your life. Good things are worth the struggle, son. How do you think she feels alone in that big house, unable to use her legs? The man she loves is nowhere to be found, and her fans have turned their backs on her. Performing is her life. Please, Mark, I beg of you to help her?"

Mark contemplates long and hard after the conversation with his mother. He comes to the realization his mother is right. China needs his help. The walls are closing in on her. He can't just stand by and let them collapse. He has to rescue her. He needs to swallow his pride and save his woman. Later in the evening, Mark packed his suitcase and placed it in the back of his Jeep Cherokee. He chooses the road over taking a flight. The drive will give him more time to plan his conversation with China. Mark enjoys the road and the smell of fresh air percolating through his nostrils. He feels safer planted in the ground than trapped in the sky. He considers how beautiful China is and how she made him feel the first time he met her. His mother is right. He needs her, and she needs him.

PAUL

21

Mr. Paul Mitchell, we, the board of Bedford Mental Institution, find that your five months of therapy have been successful. You have proven to the Bedford Mental Institution board members that you can live an everyday functioning life. To maintain your progress, a weekly visit from a therapist will further advance your development. An investigation is still pending. You may have to stand trial, and we can provide a public defender to help you. Your final day is two days from now. Good luck."

"Paul, that's great news," Alex says, trying to hide her disappointment.

"Why the long face then?"

"C'mon Paul, who will I have to talk to and look after me in this hell hole if you leave? I want out of here, too. I've tried to take my life so many times that they don't trust me alone on the outside. And besides, I have feelings for you," she looks at me, awaiting a response.

"Have you been praying and talking to God like I told you?"

"I pray three times a day. I pray morning, noon, and night. I pray for God to wipe away my fears, addiction, and suicidal impulses."

"Alexandria, I feel as strongly as you do about us. I will be here every day to visit, no matter what happens. God places people together for a reason. Your father tells me you're a good counselor. I want to start a new church. I can use a counselor for the community members who are struggling with alcohol and drug addiction."

"Saving people is hard work. The ones you try to save can end up hurting you, Paul."

"I know Alexandria, but we have to make an effort. Saving a few is better than none. I know as a team, we can change the culture of people with an addiction. Are you willing to try?"

"I will try if you let me have you," she smiles seductively.

"If you want me, you have to endure the ride. It won't be easy. I believe in celibacy until I'm married," Alexandria's mouth drops open.

"I've never met anyone celibate before. It must be hard. I mean, it's probably always hard, like right now. I mean, like when you wake up or go to bed. It must be hard every day," I shake my head and laugh.

"Woman, I get it. Very funny," she laughs with me.

"When you're serving God and keeping your mind occupied on helping others, celibacy can be a piece of cake."

"I don't mean to pry into your business, but I'm just curious how long it has been?"

"It was five years until I gave into sin."

"You deserve a medal regardless. I would've caved in a long time ago. Five years without any? I would lose my mind all over again. It might be easier to hold out when you're single, but if you're in a relationship with someone special, how do you not touch them or become intimate without damaging the bond?"

"When two people have strong feelings for each other, they should wait and do things the right way. God will bless you for it. When you don't, it complicates things. A family that prays together stays together."

"How do you feel about returning to the real world?"

"I'm ecstatic and a little worried at the same time. My situation is far from over. I will probably have to stand trial."

"But you haven't done anything; you're innocent."

"If everyone felt the same as you, I would be a free man. But unfortunately, the majority of everyone doesn't. The state of Connecticut believes I'm competent to stand trial."

"What if they find you guilty? Then what? I mean, the both of us will be devastated."

"Alexandria, you're worrying too much. God will protect us. There's nothing to worry about," I said to Alexandria with outer confidence and a few uncertainties. Deep down inside, I am afraid for my life. I have never been to jail. Even as a teen, I walked the straight and narrow. My sister made sure of it. Jail is a rite of passage in the black community. A large amount of young African-American men occupy the prisons. Having served time gives more street credibility to some needing an image. I'm past this nonsense in my life. I did everything I had to do to stay away from the penal system. I guess you can't outrun some things, and it doesn't matter how successful you become.

Bedford Mental Institution, three days prior,

Patricia sits inside her silver-tinted Toyota Camry, contemplating her next move. Bedford Mental Institution is within her sights for a third day. The first two days were frustrating without a solid plan to enter the building without being detected. Security cameras, a ten-foot barbed wire fence, and the presence of guards made her mission more difficult. She refuses to let Paul get off this easy. He must pay for his sins. The toll of sin is death. Patricia surveyed male and female staff members entering and exiting the building for the past two days. Their faces were unfamiliar to her. She needs someone to help her get inside and assist in her scheme. Discouragement begins to set in. Day three is turning out as unproductive as the previous two days. There is no one to help, mostly older men and women unable to be manipulated. The men and women look depleted and worn down from years of faithful service. Then, upon seeing her, an idea reveals itself as Francine leaves the building, heading for the parking lot.

Patricia continued her stakeout the next day but parked a few houses away from Francine's home this time. She learned a great deal of information in several weeks. Patricia discovered the grocery store

Francine attends, her favorite restaurant, and information about her significant other.

And most importantly, her steady social nightclub. Patricia lets the soothing hot water run over her body.

The steaming water relaxes her muscles. She thinks about how simple attracting men of various ages have been. Men cherished and praised her, and she received lavish gifts from them—most of the time, she never had to do anything. Men were like puppy dogs to her, doing whatever she commanded them to do. Her stepmother took interest in Patricia's looks right away. She begged her father to start Patricia off in beauty pageants at the age of fifteen. After protesting many times against it, he finally gave his approval. When she competed, the judges were astounded by her beauty and elected Patricia in every contest she contended. Men belonged to her, and she knew how to push their buttons. She studied men with fascination and made them beg for her. She gave them nothing in return. Patricia had a few partners she allowed to have sex with her, and that was it. Her partners knew how to satisfy her every desire and understood when she wanted to be left alone.

The perfect relationship, she assumes. Men were easy, but women required more cleverness. Women enjoyed challenges, spontaneity, and frequent surprises. Women need security, an everlasting commitment, and someone to trust. Francine became the weak link in destroying Paul Mitchell. Patricia studied her for several months inside of gay clubs before approaching. Francine had a Mexican lover who seemed very attached, but she gradually pulled Francine away from her. Convincing Francine that she truly loved her required doing things she had never done before. Patricia bought cards, candy, toys from VIP, and endless articles of clothing. She complimented Francine on her appearance whenever possible. Patricia made surprise visits, keeping Francine in limbo. Francine had no clue what to expect, but she relished the thrill. Patricia accessed her car, apartment, bank account, and numerous other items. Patricia's hard work had paid off. Francine shared secrets along with personal stories of her childhood. Attaining the security pass, floor plans, and different shift changes of staff made it easy for her to enter Bedford Mental Institution unnoticed.

CHINA

22

"China, you still have a life to live. I can't imagine what you're going through. I know it's difficult not to be able to walk, but there's a God who says otherwise. Just trust in him. Come back to church, and he will take care of you. I love you so much. I'm sorry for the mistakes I made as a parent. Please forgive me, China. End of message." With tears streaming down her cheeks, China throws her cell phone against the bedroom wall, almost shattering it. Suddenly, the doorbell rings, interrupting her tirade. She snaps out of her rage and then strolls down the ramp to the front door. She wants to be left alone. She hopes that they will go away if she doesn't answer. The frantic rings turn into louder knocks.

"Ms. Reynolds, are you in there? If you are, please open the door. I need to know if you're ok."

"Jason, is that you?"

"Yes, it's me."

"Give me a second, please."

"Ok," he yells back.

China ties her wild hair back into a ponytail and adjusts her lavender nightgown. She wipes her face from dried-up tears, then opens the door, letting Jason inside. He steps inside, wearing an unbuttoned white silk shirt, revealing his dark, bare chest. His pants are slightly below the waist, and his silver belt buckle dangles at his knees. China turns her attention toward his face as she recognizes he isn't wearing anything underneath. Trepidation spreads over his face. Not once has she ever seen Jason worried. He's never under pressure. His calm demeanor usually makes China feel protected.

"Ms. Reynolds, I wish you would come back to the stage. We miss you a lot."

"My life is different now. Without using my legs, it's hard to focus on singing. Jason, where's your coat? It's freezing outside," she keeps her eyes on him.

"I don't get cold. This weather feels good to me. I love the winter. How come you won't sing? All you have to do is sing, wheelchair or no wheelchair. The fans will still support you. I know I will," he replies, concentrating on her toned legs. China awkwardly stretches her nightgown over her knees.

"Jason, are you ok?"

"Sure, I'm fine. Why do you ask?"

"For starters, you're drunk and barely dressed," he ignores her question. Jason moves in closer, making her uncomfortable.

"How long have I been working for you, Ms. Reynolds?"

"I would say close to seven years," he moves in behind her.

"In all that time, have you ever thought about me?" He glides his hands over the frame of her wheelchair. China is too afraid to make any sudden movements. She continues talking.

"Jason, in all honesty, I've thought about you. When the fans are overly excited, I think about your presence being there to safeguard me," her answer is not the one he's looking for. He tries again.

"Ms. Reynolds, can I call you by your first name?" He drops his shirt on the floor right next to her. She begins to lose her composure. She grips her wheelchair tighter to stop her hands from trembling.

"It's quite alright with me. I don't have a problem with it, but can I ask you something?" She asks, struggling to get her words out.

"You can ask me anything beautiful."

"Why is your shirt off?" Jason leans over her wheelchair, smelling her hair. The scent of her hair arouses him.

"China, I'm madly in love with you. I've wanted you from the very start of my employment. I've tried giving you hints, but you never paid attention. How can you love Mark and not me? I've been with you longer, and I know everything about you. He doesn't care for you the way I do. He's not even around. I'm still here proving my love to you."

She knows Jason all too well—his temperament and how aggressive he can turn when triggered. In the past, she witnessed how he handled a few disruptive fans at some of her concerts, nearly putting each one in the hospital. Many lawsuits were pending, several of which China had to settle out of court. Jason removes his pants. China hears his belt buckle hit the floor. Her instincts tell her to stroll as fast as possible to escape him.

"Jason, can I turn around and talk to you?"

"Sure, you're more than welcome," he answers, further aroused by the thought of China observing him unclothed.

"Before I turn around, please wear your clothes so we can converse normally. If you love me the way you say you do, we can get better acquainted later. Don't you agree?" He wants to make love to her more than anything, but he also wants her to love him in return. The same way he loves her.

"Yes," he answers suspiciously, scrutinizing her movements.

"So, you feel the same way I feel?" His voice rises.

"I have for some time now, but you work for me, which would jeopardize my security."

"I knew it from the way you flirted with me. You wanted me to. You ignored my approach because of security reasons. I was so stupid not to see it. How could I miss that?" Her mind is racing. She has to come up with more lies to help her escape. "Do you love me the way I love you?" China doesn't know what to say. If she says the wrong thing, he may hurt her. *Think China, think. She utters to herself.*

"Jason, love takes time. It involves trust, commitment, and understanding. You've only been my employee. We haven't had time to build on those personal things. We need to start fresh," he grins, liking its sound.

"What would you suggest?" He asks, slowly buttoning up his shirt and then putting on his pants. Her heart rate slightly returns to normal. She maneuvers her wheelchair around to face him.

"Can I change into something more presentable than my nightgown and fix my hair at least? I will feel more relaxed talking to you if I have on something a little more appropriate."

Jason stares at her closely as his grin changes to suspicion. He scans her for any sign of deceit. Jason wants China to be his woman. He's wanted her for so long, and now he will have her. There's no one to interfere. Her former two boyfriends were easy to get rid of. China hadn't suspected anything. She assumed they left on their own accord. That was far from the truth. Jason had pressured the men into leaving her. He threatened their lives and claimed to blackmail each one if they didn't go. The scare tactics worked as they gave in to his requests. When Mark came along, Jason was fearful to try the same tactics. For one, Mark looked very intimidating. His size mattered. Jason feared that Mark might break him in two if he threatened him. In addition, China is in love with Mark. She talks of nothing but him, which makes Jason bitter. Jason even tried different strategies to get rid of him. He made anonymous calls to newspapers, telling them lies about Mark.

He falsely claimed that Mark was broke and after China's money. He also reported Mark fathered five children and owed thousands in back child support. Jason made things difficult, but Mark stuck around. When Jason discovered that Mark was jealous of her time with her fans, he did everything he could to keep her busy. Jason encouraged China to give more of herself to her fans. He pressed Kelly to contact more venues and places where China would be safe to perform. Jason even volunteered to organize autograph sessions and photo shoots in her downtime. He made it easier for her to connect with her fan base. The time-consuming sessions provided little time for Mark, eventually leading to his departure. Jason's plan had worked, but China became depressed. She yearned for Mark. After she lost her ability to walk and her relationship with Mark, she'd given up all hope. Until then, she checked in frequently with Jason over the phone, letting him know she was ok. When he didn't hear from her anymore, he became concerned. He can't afford to lose her. With Mark out of the picture, this is the time to show her how much he truly cares for her. How much he loves her and how badly he wants her.

"Can you put on something that I like?" He asks, trying to hold back his excitement.

"What would you like me to wear?"

"I have to think about it for a moment. I've seen you in so many outfits."

"I hope nothing too revealing. Remember, this is officially our first date. First impressions mean everything," China smiles at him, playing along.

"Can you wear the outfit you wore in Atlanta?"

"Jason, I've toured so many cities that I can't remember every article of clothing. Can you describe it?"

"I definitely can. It was a white mini, and you wore a pink top with pink heels. I still remember it. You blew me away that evening."

"I'm glad you liked it, but I don't think that's appropriate for a first date. I have something else in mind that I'm sure you would like. It might take a little time, though. Don't forget, I'm in a wheelchair," Jason studies her face for trickery.

"Would you like me to come up and help you?"

"That's ok, I can manage. I'm trying to be as independent as I can. I almost have this wheelchair thing down."

"Good for you. I admire you for that. How would you rate my looks from one to ten?"

"I think you're a solid eight. I don't give out tens, and nines are too close to ten. You are handsome," China says, forcing a smile.

"That means a lot to me, coming from a person with such greatness."

"Jason, all you need is confidence; you can have anyone you want."

"I don't want just anyone. I only want you. I have for a long time."

"I appreciate your kindness."

"I can't believe I'm saying these things to you. I've waited for this moment, and it is finally here. We're going to be a couple?"

"Yes, we are. I'll be down in a flash," he beams.

"China, can I use your cell phone before you get dressed? I rushed to get here and must've left my cell phone at home. I must make an important call, if you don't mind?" She wavers, thinking of something more to say.

"It's... in the kitchen, on the table," Jason notices her confusion. He heads off to the kitchen.

In Jason's field of work, he received extensive training on how to study people. It was necessary for the benefit of protecting his clients at all times. Jason had confrontations with people who would do anything to get next to China. He knew how to recognize deceptive persons. Jason had once detained a fan hiding in China's dressing room. He claimed to be maintenance, showing falsified documents that he was called in to repair the toilet. His uniform appeared legitimate. His plumbing knowledge sounded sure, and his equipment was up to par. The most crucial aspect that this imposter could not disguise was his eyes. His eyes expressed volumes of deception. His pupils roamed, trying to connect with his untruth. Jason didn't believe his story. After that, an investigation took place, and the imposter was taken into custody by the police. Jason watches as China's eyes wander in the same manner. They were roaming, looking for a way to connect with her lie.

China's heart is racing. The five mph electric wheelchair picks up acceleration. She is near the top of the ramp. After reaching the top, she turns right, facing her bedroom. Her cell phone is in her room. *Why is Jason acting this way? She trusted him to protect her. Now, China needs protection from him. She didn't see this one coming. How could she? Jason is professional. Not once did he show her anything otherwise. His drunken sexual innuendos and delusional behavior terrify her. She needs to hurry before things get worse. He will discover the truth about her cell phone. China scans the bedroom, pressing her fingers against her temple. She recalls tossing her phone against the wall. She speeds around the bedroom, searching every cubic inch. She hears Jason's voice calling her from downstairs.*

"China, the phone isn't here. Are you sure you put it on the kitchen table?" She has to stall him. She needs more time. *Where did her phone land after hitting the wall? China strolls out of her room. She stops at the top of the ramp.*

"I'm sorry, Jason. It's in the first drawer underneath the cabinets. I just remembered."

"No problem," he yells back.

"I will be down in a minute."

"Great, I'll be waiting for you."

In desperation, she strolls back to her room. She decides to look around the bed and finds nothing. She checked her nightstand, but there was still nothing. She opens her closet door, but again, nothing. China returns to her bed. But this time, she bends down forward, looking underneath it. There, to her fulfillment, below her bed lies the phone. She will have to climb out of her wheelchair to grasp it. China navigates the wheelchair beside her bed. Pressing her hands firmly against the bed to keep her balance, she turns her body around, sliding backward down the wheelchair. In her effort, she lands abruptly on the floor, bruising her chin. She winces in pain. Using her forearms and elbows to crawl under the bed, she reaches out for the phone. After attaining the phone, she crawls back out. She presses the numbers 9-1-1. He seizes the phone away from her, ending the call.

"I have to say, I'm very impressed. That took a lot of effort, but you did it. You got the phone. My call is important, but you didn't have to go through all that trouble for me. I've been standing here for the last few minutes admiring your strength," he tears off her nightgown and has his way with her.

PAUL

23

The blaring alarm disrupts my sleep. I begin preparing myself for the monthly fire drill procedure every second Wednesday. As I put on my gray robe and black slippers, I suddenly realized something other than a practice evacuation drill was occurring because today was only Friday. The atmosphere outside my room sounds chaotic. I venture out of my tiny living quarters to see what is happening.

Patients have left their rooms. I'm baffled, along with others, as to why the alarm is sounding. Harold heads in my direction.

"Paul, is there an evacuation drill today?" He asks.

"There shouldn't be. Today is Friday evening. It's always the third Wednesday of each month in the morning."

"Well, maybe they changed it."

"Maybe, but I doubt it. Bedford follows strict policy."

"Harold, have you seen Alex?"

"No, I haven't? Have you tried her room?"

"No, but I think I will visit her. Something doesn't feel right to me."

"Aren't you leaving here soon?"

"That's what they tell me, but you never know what can happen in a few days. They can change their mind."

"I wish I was leaving in a few days. I miss my family. I served my country for twenty years, fighting in senseless wars. I killed men with my bare hands and with weapons. I thought I left the war on the battlefield, but the war has carried over inside my head. My family brought me here because I can hear voices. The voices tell me violent things. Sometimes, the voices instruct me to kill myself. Sometimes, the voices tell me to kill others. Without my medicine, I don't think I would be able to control it. When the voices are inside my head, it hurts a lot. I want to stop the pain by doing whatever the voices are influencing me to do. I figure I will be realizing for the rest of my life," Harold sighs. I try to comfort him.

"Do you believe in God, Harold?" He looks into my eyes and changes his solemn demeanor.

"I did a very long time ago. I stopped believing because God never answered me. I wasted my time praying and going to church. I prayed for him to take away my sickness, and he's done nothing. My prayers go unanswered. I have given up on him. God has given up on me. It looks to me that he's given up on you too. You're a pastor of the church. Why isn't he here for you?"

"The Bible tells us our faith is stronger through trials and tribulations. For God to intervene, we must stand strong and refuse to let adversity break us. If we continue to pray and ask for God's help, he will answer our prayers. You must first pass the test. He will not give us any more than we can handle," he shakes his head in disgust.

"Paul, you know something?"

"Know what?"

"The words always sound easy, but life is difficult. Words cannot remove the voices from my head. I need something of substance."

"The words are substance. Just lean on God and believe he will save you. And he will."

"Do you honestly believe in this?"

"I certainly do, but I've turned away from God." in recent months,

"What happened?"

"I'm here because of a woman," I say with embarrassment. "I allowed her to pull me away from God. I became distracted by her. Have you ever been crazy for a woman to the point of doing anything to be with her?"

"She went by the name of Candy."

"Candy?"

"That's what all the guys in high school called her. She looked sweet as candy, and everyone worshipped her like a goddess. Her real name is Candice Jackson. I think she loved it when we called her candy. She never permitted any boy to get close to her without sneering at them. I had a serious crush on Candy. Whenever she came around, I couldn't talk, think, or act normal. When school ended, I counted the hours until the next school day. I stood by her classroom every morning to see her walk in. She was the total package."

"I can relate," I chuckle.

"One day, I made it my business to approach her. I was determined to get my girl."

"So, what did you do?"

"I walked straight over to her in the crowded lunchroom. My words almost didn't come out. I told her she was the prettiest girl I'd ever seen. She stopped eating and ignored her girlfriend, giggling when she heard what I said. She said she thought I was handsome as well. The rest is history."

"What do you mean the rest is history?"

"I married her."

"Wow, Harold, impressive. You married your high school sweetheart? I'm jealous."

"She's been there for me ever since. The perfect wife, she's never left my side."

"I don't know what to say."

"Don't say anything. When your special someone comes along, everything will feel picture-perfect. You won't have a care in the world. I think today is your test."

"Why do you say that?"

"Here comes staff, and I don't think they're happy," the three staff members push their way through the crowd of patients, with Curtis leading the way. They surround me.

Harold intervenes, stepping in front of me.

"What is this about fellas?" Harold clenches his big hands together.

"It's none of your concern, Harold. Stay out of our way."

"I feel otherwise. Paul is a friend of mine. I think I have a right to know."

"I tell you what!" Curtis yells back. "If you don't move out of our way, I will take you down and put you in solitary confinement."

It doesn't take long for Harold to strike Curtis across the face. The tension between the two was everlasting. Harold is a big, burly man who still has a lot of fight left in him to be a senior citizen. He throws a punch, reminding me of a seasoned George Forman hitting a younger Larry Holmes. The solid force sends Curtis plummeting to the floor. This action by Harold doesn't sit too well with the other staff members. Maurice, the nicest of the three and by far the biggest, stands six feet five and is shaped like a linebacker with a shiny bald head. He bends down slightly, gaining momentum, and rams his right shoulder into Harold's chest. The force lifts Harold off his feet. Harold lands hard. I extend my hand to help my hip, but Ricky grabs my arms, twisting them behind my back. I can feel the sharp pain in both shoulders. Curtis gets back to his feet. He starts kicking Harold repeatedly while cursing at him. Maurice joins in. Harold balls into a fetal position. He pulls in both knees, covering his midsection. His hands are protecting his head and face. Ricky has a resilient hold on my arms.

He isn't as big as Maurice, fatter, and strong as an ox. I try to free myself. My attempt was unsuccessful. The other patients intrude. There is now bedlam in Bedford. The small mob of patients ascend to our rescue, forming a circle around us. Bryson charges from the crowd. He jumps on Maurice's back, clasping his neck. Maurice tumbles, losing his balance. The others follow suit. He is under attack. The patients distribute an arsenal of kicks and punches to his body. Maurice tries to crawl to freedom, but Bryson stiffens his hold. The patients yank Maurice back to the floor, continuing their attack. Curtis tries to help. Too many patients overtake him. The gatekeeper activates the alarm, screaming for help. In all the mayhem, I manage to elude my captor. My right arm is free. I send an uppercut to Ricky's chin. He drops instantaneously. I run over to get Curtis away from Harold. Then, out of nowhere, before I can react, an object strikes me. I feel the sharp blow to my temple. I stagger and drop. The room blackens.

My whereabouts are unknown to me. I don't know how long I've been here. My head is pounding. Whoever struck me from behind made sure I wasn't moving. The knot above my temple feels like a golf ball. I try to stand, but shackles tug my body back to the cold, cemented floor. My hands and feet are chained together. A chain around my waist is attached to what feels like a brick wall. I am unable to see. The cold room is dark. They have stripped me of my clothing. I hear screams. I am inside a torture chamber. Alexandria said it existed. I never believed her. How can rooms like this one still exist in the twentieth century? I hear a door open. Light entering from the outside blinds me. Footsteps approach fast. I cling against the wall, not knowing what to expect. My lips are trembling. Frostbite has taken over my hands and feet. The footsteps stop. I smell the scent of his horrible cologne.

"Paul, why have you done this to yourself? You were leaving here in a couple of days. I don't understand your actions."

"They treated Harold like an animal. He's a human being. We all are human beings. We deserve respect just like anyone else. Just because we're in here doesn't give you the right to treat us with contempt," I answer him, shivering.

"Curtis, go cover him up with this blanket. We don't want him dying on us before we have our fun," I cling to the warm quilt. "To get respect, you have to earn it. Harold is far from a saint. He hit a staff member and paid the price for it."

"He was only protecting me. Curtis should be punished, not us."

"We know you did it, Paul, you sick freak," Curtis protests.

"Paul, you have put yourself in a terrible quandary."

"For protecting a friend? I would do it again and again if I had to. Ricky, let me ask you something: how did that uppercut feel?" Ricky charges toward me and slaps me. The pain reemerges. I want to scream, but I must show strength in their presence. I will not show them any signs of weakness.

"You're going to pay for this, Paul. I'll see to it personally."

"Ricky, that's enough. Step back at once!"

"Doc, why are we talking to him? After what he's done, he deserves to pay with his life."

"Soon, Ricky, you'll have your chance. We will all have our chance."

"Pay with my life for protecting a friend?" I ask as my eyes begin to adjust to the outside light. "I have rights. I demand you unchain me and let me out of this room!"

"You're in no position to make demands. I have seen your handy work, and I must say I misjudged you. Having twelve years of counseling, I can usually detect certain flaws in a patient's character. You mislead me. I honestly believed in your sincerity."

"Why would I mislead you? I told you the truth. I am a man of God. There's no reason for me to lie."

"How do you feel about Alexandria?" His voice is stern. I can see each of them now more clearly. Ricky is fuming. He is pacing around the room. Curtis is behind the doctor, holding a briefcase in his right hand. Maurice is standing over what appears to be a large plastic bag.

"Alexandria is a good friend. Over the past few months, our relationship has developed into something meaningful."

"So, would you say you have a way with women?"

"If you're referring to me as a lady's man, that is not who I am. I respect women. What are you getting at, doctor?"

"The same way you respected Patricia?"

"I will not answer that question. You know what type of person I am."

"Do I, Paul?" He rubs his scar. "Why did you do it?"

"I was protecting Harold."

"Doc, let me have ten minutes alone with him," Ricky pleads.

"I said no, Ricky, not now. His time is almost up. It all depends on Mr. Paul's honesty."

"Look, doc, I don't know what type of game you're playing, but I don't like it. Let me loose. I have rights. Respect my rights!"

"Respect your rights?" He shouts at me. "Did you respect Patricia or Alexandria? I know you wanted her, Paul. Everyone in here can attest to that. We saw how the two of you were constantly together." *My blood is spilling over, but not to the point of warming my frozen hands and feet. I try to stay calm as possible to avoid another panic attack.*

"We only talked and helped each other through our problems. Alexandria and I connected as counselors," he laughs at my statement.

"She told you she was a counselor?" The good, the bad, and the ugly find it very amusing. They break out in laughter.

"Yes, a drug and alcohol counselor. Why all the laughter?"

"Mr. Paul, Mr. Paul, Mr. Paul. You have a lot to learn about Bedford. Every patient in Bedford is here for a special reason. Alexandria is a pathological liar. She has many personality traits. A few of which I'm sure you've already met. Her family believes in her wholeheartedly. Her poor dad thinks Alexandria is harmless. Alexandria is the one dishing out the harm on everyone else. Did her father tell you how Alexandria lost everything when she met Andy?"

"Yes, he did. Why do you ask?"

"The story is backward. Andy lost everything when he met Alexandria. Alexandria lied to Andy. She stole from him, and she introduced him to drugs."

"How do you know this for sure?" *I know he's lying. He will say or do anything to protect himself. He wants Alexandria.*

"Her favorite personality type, and by far the most persuasive, is when she acts like a high-class prostitute named Sandy. Has she ever tried to seduce you?"

"No, we have a great friendship and a strong bond." *She did ask to have me, but that was different.*

"I don't believe you."

"What is there not to believe?"

"Alexandria has a way of convincing men to give in to her. Isn't that right, Ricky?" He refuses to make eye contact with the doctor. He doesn't respond and ignores the question. "She did a masterful job of deceiving him. In a couple of months, she was able to control him entirely. She seduced him mentally, physically, and emotionally. When she told Ricky it was over, he fell apart. As staff, we are not allowed to get involved with patients, but Alexandria made this rule hard to abide by. He lost twenty pounds in a month. He was damaged goods. Whenever he comes into contact with her, he's a nervous wreck."

"You're lying to me. I don't believe any of it."

"So you think I'm making this up? Let me enlighten you, Paul. Alex loves control. She finds delight in watching men make a fool of their selves for her. She's harmless if you do what she wants, but never go against her. I found out the hard way. Remember when you asked me about my scar? Well, Alexandria left her mark on me."

"That's not the truth. Alex admitted you were after her. She was afraid of you. In her therapy sessions, you made her sit close to you. You couldn't get enough of her!"

"Is that what you think, Mr. Paul? He asks cynically.

"Alexandria had to be strapped in her chair with two staff members present. She tried to lure me in just like Ricky. I'm her doctor. I told her no. She didn't take it lightly. A few weeks later, she came by my office for another session. When I opened the door, Alexandria used a knife to slice my face, which she had confiscated from one of the visitor's pockets. She carved the letter c into my face, which damaged a few nerves. C is for Charles, my middle name. Dr. Raymond Charles Osborne. Now, do I have your attention? Don't play dumb. You know what you did. How did you do it, and why did you do it? And before we find out the real reason behind your malicious act, we will give you something to remember. A reminder of what will happen just in case you ever try this stunt again."

DAVID

24

The phone call a few days ago from Keisha Brown caught David by surprise. "Your uncle died this morning," her words, still etched in his memory, are hard to swallow. Chuck had done a great job replacing his deceased father. He was a genuine role model who taught David many valuable life lessons. He battled with cancer as long as he could before succumbing to it. The tumor spread immediately throughout his lungs. Chuck smoked a pack of cigarettes for most of his life, always promising to quit, but he never gave in. At no time did he ever back down from a fight, except with nicotine. As the plane cruises over Montreal, Canada, into the United States, David envisions death. He is beginning to understand its true meaning. During the period his grandmother passed away, David had a difficult time adjusting. His grandmother's manifestation as she lay dead on the carpet confused him for many years until now. He observed the various faces at her funeral. Some were grieved stricken and poured their hearts out for his grandmother, who would never walk this earth again. Family members, friends, and coworkers disbelieve entirely. Crying irrepressibly for their loss and realizing one day, their fate would also come. His grandmother's countenance was one of peacefulness. She didn't seem dead to David. She appeared to be resting in a deep sleep to rejuvenate her body.

As the turbulence shakes the Delta Airliner, David holds onto his seat and smiles. He understands that true harmony must come from death. The living is repeatedly suffering while the dead have moved on. David desires to end his uncertainties and lessen his despair. He wants to feel the ultimate peace. The petite Asian escort holds David's hand as they enter the airport. Keisha Brown stands at the end of the terminal, holding a sign displaying David's name. The escort tells David she is a big fan of his. She asks for his autograph before leaving. He kindly signs her pocket-size notebook. She thanked David and handed him to Keisha. David feels the roughness of Keisha's hands. Her fingernails are almost nonexistent from biting them. She smells like an ashtray. He wonders how long before cancer will grip her, too.

"David, how are you doing?"

"Not good, Keisha, but I'm surviving."

"Well, that's good to hear. You've always been strong, even when you were little. Chuck cared so much for you," her voice cracks.

"Are you ok, Keisha?"

"I'll be fine. It's just that I've been with your uncle for so many years. I don't know anything but him. He was a good man. The best man I've ever had. He treated me like royalty. I will miss him."

"We will both miss him. He taught me a lot about life. I don't think I would be the man I am today if it wasn't for him. He gave me courage. He taught me how to be a man."

"I was with him until the end. I stayed with him day and night, and you know something, David? His last words were for you."

"For me?"

"He wanted you to know he is finally at rest and not to worry about him."

"Don't you think it's better to be dead than alive?" Keisha stops walking. She lets go of David's hand. She folds her arms together, and her soft brown eyes glare at him.

"Why would anyone want to be dead, David?"

"The dead are free. No more problems to deal with. No more stress and pure blissfulness."

"David, how can you say that? Is it a blessing to receive life? It is better to live than to not have lived at all. Life is full of happy memories and good times. We carry these celebrations with us each day. They keep us moving forward."

"What about when bad memories pile on with more and more problems? How do we keep moving on in the face of hardship?" Keisha clutches David by the arm.

"David, I know where you're heading. Please, I beg of you, don't take that route. Things will always come to us in life, whether good or bad. We have no choice; this is the price of living. You came into this world free of charge. But you have so much to live for. You are truly a blessed person."

"I don't feel blessed. I feel cursed."

"You're a miracle walking. We're all miracles. To live each day with so many things that can take us out is a miracle. You can't see it because you've had some disappointments happen in your life. But for you to stand here is a miracle. Sometimes, when I'm home, I watch that nerve-wracking show. It's called "A Thousand Ways to Die". I'm sure you've seen it before.

"Yes, I have."

"Well, to see regular people die at any time in their life is spine-chilling to me. They're happy one minute, and their life is over the next. We have no control over it. We can only live and enjoy the moments that we have. Chuck would be very disappointed in you if you gave up. He wasn't a quitter. He was a fighter. He fought to the end and would've expected the same thing from his only nephew."

"It's tough for me, Keisha. I feel helpless and not accustomed to people waiting on me. I've always been self-sufficient. It angers me to have people take care of me. I don't want to live in darkness anymore. I want to be free. Free from this world and all the problems that go along with it."

"David, I'm not a preacher, a priest, or a pope. I'm not even very religious. But I do believe in God. I believe in faith and prayer. You can't give up on hope. Not just yet. You have to fight the fight and walk the walk. Put your energies into helping others. They're people who are struggling even more than you. I know you're without sight, but I believe deep in my heart you can save someone. Chuck dedicated his life to helping kids. He wasn't perfect. He was far from a saint, but with all his issues, he still managed to coach inner-city youth. The youth saw his perfection on the field and never noticed his flaws. The only way you'll be able to live with this is to put your focus on others."

"How can I focus on helping others when I can't help myself? I just want to die!" David slams his hands against the dashboard.

"Hey, what are you doing?" Keisha yells. My car isn't new, but it gets me from A to B. Please be careful. I'm not rich."

"My bad, I'm sorry. I won't do it again," Keisha shakes her head in disgust.

"David, that's enough talk about death. We're burying Chuck in a couple of days. Let's enjoy the rest of the evening on a positive note. I cooked before I left. My food will make you feel better."

"I guess I can't argue with that. I haven't had good home cooking in a very long time."

The drive from the airport doesn't take long. Keisha maneuvers her blue Honda Accord like a speed demon. She swerves in and out of lanes, angering other motorists. David hears the horns blaring as she makes inappropriate lane changes on I-95, cursing at the drivers she offends. The last time David was in New Haven Ct. was right before he entered the CFL draft. He remembers the city and how violent it had become before he left. The violence has turned threefold since his departure. Shootings occur on a day-to-day basis, leading to many deaths of young black men. The violence has residents living on the edge. New Haven has developed into a war zone. When traveling, many of its citizens take precautionary measures to stay away from troubling areas during the day and the late night hours. New Haven, on average, totals at least thirty-five gun-related deaths per year.

The mayor's grade on solving the town's gun violence issue ranks as a disappointing "f." Political leaders, civil rights advocates, local police, and those residing in New Haven are doing absolutely nothing to correct the problem. A statistical analysis highlights Elm City as the fourth most violent city in the nation, harboring a meager one hundred thirty thousand people. David wonders how Yale University can prosper in the center of the town and cares nothing about the young men dying right next door. Keisha pulls hard to the right, slamming on her brakes. David is thrown forward and is thankful the seatbelt works.

"Well, David, we're here."

"That was fast. You can wheel a car."

"Chuck used to complain about my driving. He said one day I might end up dead in a car accident."

"He was right. You need to slow down a bit."

"I know, but I hate the traffic. When I'm going somewhere, I want to get there."

"I hear that, but you might end up on "A Thousand Ways to Die," they both laugh. The apartment smells the same to David. It smells like stale cigarettes with a pungent stench of Comet cleaner. He speculates it looks the same also.

"Keisha, I know you want to ensure I don't bump into anything, but can I walk around the apartment alone?"

"Do you think that's safe, David? What if you fall?"

"I remember every inch of this place. Uncle Chuck and I had a lot of good times here. Is there anything different that I should know about?"

"Not really, you know your uncle. He held onto everything. He was a true hoarder. Everything is still in its original place. Just be careful. I don't want you scaring me half to death."

"Keisha, how is Nate doing these days?"

"He's fine, I guess, getting on my damn nerves. I wish he'd gone to college like you did. He's a grown man and still begging me for money. He should be giving me money after all I've wasted on him. His main problem is women. He's always shacking up with this one and that one.

He lets the good ones go and keeps the trash. I'll never understand that boy. You sure you don't want me to help you walk around the house?"

"I got this. If I fall, I fall. I should be alright."

"Okay, I will wash my hands to heat the dinner. Be careful now."

"Stop worrying, Keisha. Nothing is going to happen."

David outspreads his arms to feel for the walls in the corridor leading to the other rooms. He walks tentatively through the two-bedroom apartment, letting the off-white walls guide his baby steps. The blueprint of the apartment is in his memory. The kitchen to the right and a small bathroom to the left are at the end of the shortened corridor. He walks into the kitchen. His nostrils get a succulent aroma from sirloin steak, mashed potatoes, and corn on the cob. He then touches the refrigerator in the left corner, sizing up the distance to the middle of the floor. He's confident the thirty-eight special is in the middle of the flooring. He gets on his knees and begins to crawl. He hits each tile with minor pressure and attempts to feel for the steel covering. David edges in closer and closer, sensing he's near the significant tile. He must hurry before Keisha returns. Dropping his right fist, he hits another tile again and hears the familiar hollow sound and footsteps rushing into the kitchen.

"David, are you alright?" Keisha bends down to help him.

"I'm fine, Keisha. I just slipped, but I'm ok."

"I should've never let you walk by yourself inside the apartment. Your uncle would've killed me if he was still alive. Forgive me."

"I'm fine. There are no broken bones," Keisha grabs him by the arm and helps him off the floor. While getting up, David bumps his head on the corner of the table.

"The table, it wasn't here before, right?" David rubs his sore head.

"Oops, I forgot to mention it. I wanted that thing so bad when I first laid eyes on it. I begged your uncle to get it for us. He didn't like it. He wanted to keep that raggedy little worn-out two-seat table we had for years. This table's texture is so much better. It's nice and sturdy. It makes the kitchen come to life. Touch it; doesn't it feel perfect?"

"I must admit, it's very smooth and hard, too," Keisha cracks up, showing her age. She isn't as striking as in her thirties, but her sixty-ish smile is appealing.

Keisha helps David to sit at the table. He can't wait to sink his teeth in a home-cooked meal primed and prepped by an expert in the kitchen. Keisha knows how to make more than a sandwich. Mealtime was plentiful for David and his uncle. Her dinners were delicious. As David wolfs down his food, he focuses on the tile flooring. *He wonders if the gun is there or if it's loaded. Does it fire? Only time will tell. How ironic, he thinks. He doesn't believe in God or the bible, but the Last Supper pops into his head—Jesus's last dinner before being crucified. David intends to make this his last meal before taking his meaningless life.*

PAUL

25

Six hours ago, Patricia Martin had driven to Bedford Mental Institution to execute her plan. How successful was her project? She had no idea. Not until she makes contact with Francine. When she entered the asylum, the patients were asleep. Francine had previously informed her that most third-shift staff never stayed awake. They often dosed off and tried to cover for one another. The graveyard shift enticed employees because it paid more for late morning hours. Francine had once worked the graveyard shift to help purchase a new car. She complained of how tired she felt throughout the night, even when going to bed on time. Francine told Patricia that human beings should not work at unreasonable night hours, and their circadian rhythms need rest during this time. Francine called it the zombie shift. It was Brain functioning at a limited capacity. Before Patricia started her 3 am mission, she did a few practice runs to eliminate any mistakes or surprises. She knew precisely where to go and what to do. If something went wrong, Patricia had several backup plans in place. She wears a black waterproof outfit comparable to scuba gear with rubber boots, a mask, and a nap sack. Patricia shuffles through a cold, dense forest and odorous sludge to reach the asylum. She enters the grounds from the rear using a wire cutter to make a large enough hole for a crawlspace. Patricia had previously learned there weren't any cameras in this area of the asylum but looked out for personnel cautiously. She proceeds to a hidden trap door covered with artificial grass leading to a basement area. Reaching into her knapsack, she pulls out a small flashlight and opens the trap door ascending down the constricted stairwell. Halfway down the stairs, a noise jolts her. She stops her movement. On her previous runs, things were pretty quiet. As she listens more closely, the noise sounds like a moan, a painful cry. She doesn't have time to investigate. The patients will soon awaken. Her intuition keeps nagging her, but she shrugs off and continues her assignment. A pungent stench of mildew and human flesh nips at her nostrils. Patricia overlooks her worry, telling herself not to be afraid. The word fear has no place in her vocabulary. Patricia backed down from no one, not even the pimp that abused her mother.

Patricia grew up in the metropolitan area of Bridgeport, Connecticut. Her mother was a prostitute. Octavia Smith preserved her secret from Patricia as long as time would permit. She wanted Patricia to have the best things money could buy. With limited education from dropping out of school at thirteen, she did whatever she could to make her daughter happy. Octavia had regulars who would visit her during all-night hours. She hates the pimp she works for, but without him, her chance of taking care of Patricia is very slim. Devon Jones said fate brought them together, reminding her often.

"Tavia, you know if you had never run away, I would've never been the man I am today. You inspired me to be all I can be. When I first saw you, I knew you were beautiful. Few women out there had the looks that you had. You know what I'm saying? You were young, vivacious, shapely, and had the fattest backside from her to Georgia. You had the equipment, and I had the finances. When I first put you out there to trick, the men nearly lost their minds. They called me day in and day out so they could have a piece of you. Every husband, politician, doctor, and lawyer seemed to have the hots for you. When that happened, I found more girls. Girls like you. Well, close to you anyway. It made my business grow. I became successful. Not only from prostitution but from drugs and liquor as well. I'm a damn entrepreneur, and I'm proud of it."

Octavia remains quiet. She thinks of how Devon swindled her at the age of thirteen and promised her the world, never providing anything. He fed her to the wolves instead, wolves in sheep's clothing.

She was introduced to lustful husbands unfaithful to their wives, dirty politicians lying to their constituents while indulging in prostitution and drugs, reputable doctors who laid their hands in forbidden places, and a slew of crooked lawyers searching for the truth in court while living their lie outside of court. She had been with them all. It never mattered that she was thirteen. The perverted men wanted her even more. Her innocence made her desirable. Octavia's eyes ascend from his polished leather shoes and white suit to his tight interweaved corn rolls. She looks into his hardened, unlawful façade and can't imagine having ever loved this man. But she had; she had once loved him entirely. He was the perfect gentleman in the beginning. He protected her from harm and supported her decisions. Devon gave Octavia the needed attention she desired. He rubbed her back and massaged her feet with the softest hands. His kisses were passionate. His lovemaking was tender. When Devon proposed to her, she accepted without hesitation. He became her king, and in return, she became his queen. Devon saved her from a failed adolescence. Then, without warning, he changed. His soft hands turned into weapons of mass destruction. He beat her. He lashed out at her if she didn't prepare his meals on time. He tripled her load of clients and confiscated most of her money.

He punished her whenever he saw the need to. He left marks and bruises on her body. Tonight, Octavia fears for her life. Her money for the week is inadequate. Devon will make her pay it one way or another. The living room holds a loveseat and an old, worn-out recliner. It was the first two things he'd purchased for her when he gave Octavia the keys to the apartment so many years ago. They made love so frequently on the loveseat that the springs squeaked. It was a time when he cherished her and a time when she meant more to him than money. Octavia rises from the loveseat as the squeaky springs ring out. She unwillingly walks over to Devon, handing him the money she made for the week. He slaps her rear end and then counts the cash. He throws the money on the living room carpet when he finishes counting.

"Tavia, are you holding out on me?" Devon leers at her.

"This is all I made this week. Some of my regulars canceled. I'll make it up next week. I promise."

"You promise? Am I supposed to wait next week for my money? I'm a businessman. I have things to take care of. I need my profit, Goddammit!" Octavia looks weary. Her insides ache, and her ankles swollen. She can't withstand another beating from Devon.

"Please, Devon, calm down. You'll wake up Patricia. I promise I'll get your money."

"You want me to be quiet for a bastard child you had by one of your clients? What did I tell you from the start? I told you to make them use protection. But no, you thought this white cracker would take you in and marry you. Didn't you? You're just a piece of ass to him."

"He loves me, Devon, and I love him. He makes me feel special. He treats me well," her mouth quivers.

"Then where is he? He will never bring you into his world. His family would disapprove of it. You're just a whore, and that's all you'll ever be. So get that love idea out of your head. The only thing you better be thinking about is my money. I told you how I am about my money. But you don't listen very well, do you, Tavia? I'm about to make you listen loud and clear!" Devon storms off to the kitchen, looking for anything to reprimand her.

"Mama, are you alright?" Patricia whispers from her doorway, standing in her flower-designed pajamas.

"Go back to bed, baby, momma's fine. Devon and I are just arguing; that's all."

"Why are you crying?"

"I'm not crying, girl. I have allergies. They make my eyes water. Now, you go back to bed before Devon catches you up."

"He's not my father. I don't have to listen to him."

"But you have to listen to me. I said go to bed, hurry up!"

"Mamma, I know he's been beating you, and I know about the men taking advantage of you."

"Lord Jesus, help me," Octavia cries out, placing her head into her hands.

"Mama, don't be ashamed. I know you do this for me. I love you, mama," Octavia said, walking over to Patricia and hugging her tightly.

"You a good daughter, Patricia, and bright. I want you to go to school and be somebody. I don't ever want you to live like I've lived. Men are pigs, Patricia, just plain pigs. They use us and then throw us away. Never let a man use you, and never let a man throw you away."

"So what is this, family hour? Little girl, I think it's time for you to go back to sleep," Devon commands.

"You're not my daddy. You're just a bum. A man pretending to be someone he's not while stealing from people."

"Patricia! Octavia yells, grabbing her by the shoulders. Respect your elders."

"He doesn't deserve my respect, mama. He beats you every night for no reason. I'm not afraid of him, and he doesn't scare me. I hate him!" Octavia keeps her eyes on Devon, fearing for the worst.

"He's done a lot for us. Without him, we wouldn't have anywhere to live. He took me in when I was a little older than you and had nowhere to go."

"We can make it without him, mama. We don't need a man like him."

"You just gonna stand there and let that little bitch talk to me like that?" Devon clenches the handle of the sharp butcher knife behind his back.

"Honey, go back to bed. You need to get some rest; it's late."

"If I go back to bed, he will hurt you like he always does," she scowled at Devon. Devon takes warning from Patricia's menacing stare. The child is only ten, but her eyes foreshadow a wild rage. Devon is associated with thugs and gangsters of his kind. He met his share of sinister people and persons liable to cut your throat if owed a dollar. Their rage was often unreasonable but necessary to keep their reputation intact. Patricia stands in her bedroom doorway with the same anger—a warning of what will come.

"It'll be alright, baby. Mama will be fine. Sometimes people argue when they love each other."

"Love isn't supposed to hurt. He hurts you. How can he love you and hurt you the way he does? That's not love, mama, that's pain."

"Tavia, I've had enough of her already. Get her out of my sight, or I'll move her myself," Octavia shudders.

"Come move me," Patricia screams at him. Devon reveals the butcher knife. Octavia stands in front of Patricia, shielding her on wobbly legs.

"You will not touch her. You hear me? She's my child, Devon."

"Your child needs some discipline. Since you can't control her, I'll take care of it. A good ass whooping will put her in line."

"You will not touch her, I said."

"And if I do?" He chuckles.

"Then, you'll have to deal with me," the words barely escape her lips.

"Well, Tavia, I guess I got two asses to whoop. You two will respect me from now on."

Patricia stands behind her mother. Her arms wrapped around Octavia's waist, and her cheeks pressed against her back. She can feel the damp moisture from nervous perspiration through her mother's shirt. Her mother's heartbeat is a frantic drubbing. Octavia realizes she must get the knife out of his hand. It is the only way to stop him from hurting them both. How can she do it? She can hardly stand on swollen ankles—her tired body aches. The constant abuse by men and the agonizing beatings she receives from Devon hinder her mobility. Octavia will not allow Devon or any man to put their hands on Patricia. An idea has to present itself, a solution to their current fate. She closes her eyes briefly, asking God to send her a miracle. *Lord, just help me this once, and I will live a better life. I will live a better life for you and my child. I promise."*

"Who wants their ass whooped first? Is it you, Tavia? You know how we get down. Let your daughter see what happens when a woman refuses to obey a man," Devon starts to remove his jacket. He puts the knife in his left hand and proceeds to remove his right arm from the right sleeve. Octavia doesn't waste her opportunity. She unlatches Patricia's arms, dashing forward. Devon's eyes widen. He tries to get the knife back into his right hand. Octavia swings wildly. She succeeds by hitting the knife handle. The blade drops to the carpet. They both dive for the knife. Octavia is closer to the knife. She reaches out to grab it. Devon latches his jacket around her throat, dragging her back. He then twists the jacket, cutting off her oxygen. She pants and kicks, flapping her arms to free herself. Her fists swing blindly, missing his entire face. He exchanges his position to stay out of her reach. He Plants his right knee in her back and prevents her body from rising. Devon's strength is too much for her. He coils the jacket tighter. Her light is fading. Her world is getting darker.

Asphyxiation is setting in, and her gasps become less. Her kicks slow down, and her arms lie frozen. Octavia envisions her demise. How will Patricia survive without her? She cannot leave her child, not in the hands of this monster. He will corrupt her and turn her into a woman of the night. She will become a woman with many lovers. Men who want to experience pleasure on a different level. A level unaccustomed to their wives. Patricia will grow to hate men and what they stand for. Her efforts to escape fail. She continues to try, but it's hopeless. She decides it's much easier to give in to death than to struggle. Then, without warning, she hears an outcry. A loud yell from Devon delays her grave. Her strangulation ends. Octavia coughs and massages her throat to stop the burning. She inhales profoundly, letting the oxygen return to her lungs.

Octavia can move but only partially. She removes the white jacket around her neck, flinging it to the side. When the coat falls against the carpet, it has stained crimson red that has mixed in. Alarmed, she tries in earnest to turn over. The extra mass makes it difficult. His body is lying on top of her. She detects movement even though he lies lifeless. The action is a persistent pulse. With little strength, she manages to roll Devon off of her. Blood streams out of his corpse into the Oriental rug. In complete shock, she turns to Patricia, holding the butcher knife in both hands. His blood stains her face as the blade rises and falls again and again.

"Baby, please give me the knife. He's dead now. He can no longer hurt us," Patricia continues, wielding the butcher knife with trembling hands. She is transfixed on her purpose and stabs violently onto the carpet.

"Patricia! Octavia bellows out, but her call goes unnoticed. The carpet filaments begin to separate. A small hole begins to form. Octavia gets next to Patricia and folds her arms around her small, unstable body. She prevents the knife from further damage and carefully takes it away from Patricia. Patricia is shaking terribly. It's ok, baby, I'm here. Let it go, honey. Let go of the knife. He's gone now. He's gone and never coming back."

Back inside the asylum, Patricia sits at the top stairwell and removes her outer clothing, placing it in her knapsack. She is wearing a black body suit. She slides Francine's key card into the thin white slot bordering the door. The green light activates a short beep. Turning the door handle with caution, she cracks open the door. The stillness of the first floor is a soundless cemetery after sundown. Patricia peers out, looking for the rotating camera at the end of the hall. She times the camera's rotation. Sprinting as fast as her legs permit, she runs in route of the camera, ducking below its visibility. Patricia takes off the rubber band, holding her ponytail in place, and uses it to jam the camera, preventing it from full rotation. Now that the camera's right side is inoperable, she treads down the hallway to the left. As Patricia nears Francine's work area, Patricia spots the guard's wilted body sprawled out against the desk in a deep sleep. Patricia continues onward to her endpoint, examining each room she passes. Patricia slides the key card into a second door, awaiting the green light, and then opens the room door, confiscating some items. She further moves down the hallway, approaching a third door. Once inside, the adrenaline rush from vengeance prompts her to carry out her malicious undertaking. The small rectangular room has a bed, a tiny stainless steel toilet, and numerous handmade drawings pasted alongside the wall. One picture stands out more than the others. Patricia's engaged by it. It's a replica of her nemesis. The eyes are similar, and the features are equal in comparison. It's as if Paul Mitchel is there watching her every move. The drawing generates an irrepressible rage. She then jumps atop the resting body, restraining from movement. She uses the pillow to smother it.

An unnerving chill grows inside of me. I worry, but my great concern is not exclusively for myself alone. I can tolerate whatever the doctor dishes out. God will protect me. He always has. He only gives me what I can handle. Most of my apprehension originates from the large bag in front of Maurice. Ricky is seething. He is unable to calm himself. He wants to tear me apart, but the doctor will not allow him. The doctor's derisive inquiries and the staff's detestable expressions lead me to believe something other than a fight has put me here.

"Do you have anything to say before I hand out my swift justice?" The doctor asks.

"Who made you judge, jury, and executioner? I haven't done anything wrong. I'm innocent until proven guilty in a court of law."

"You say you haven't done anything wrong, but the content in this bag tells us a different story. Your room door was the only one open last night. The evidence is all here. There's no need for a jury to screw things up. I run this asylum. I make the rules. I have the final say in every matter. I transform those that society has given up on. This chamber is where my justice takes place. It took years to build this chamber. I take great pride in disciplining my patients."

"You will never get away with this. My sister will look for me. She will ask questions," unfazed by my comment, he continues his tirade.

"My father taught me a painful but valuable lesson many years ago. He was a strict disciplinarian. My siblings and I suffered many nights at the hands of my father. We were never allowed to be disobedient. If one of us stepped out of line, he reminded us quickly he was always in charge. My siblings and I feared him. We never knew what to expect. As the years passed, we began to figure it out. It all depended on the severity of our behavior."

"What does this have to do with me? It's irrelevant. Free me at once. You don't have the right to hold me in chains. I'm a human being, not an animal!" Again, he ignores my plea.

"Cutting up in school was high on the list of things not to do. Once, my brother decided to skip school and hang out with his friends. Later on that evening, my father learned of it from school officials. My siblings and I thought he would kill our brother. He whipped him for so long I can still hear his screams from years past. He had a special area in the house designated for punishment. My father would drag the defiant sibling down to the cellar. There were special tools designed to punish us. When he whipped my brother for skipping school, he used a whip exactly like the ones used to tame circus animals. I hated my father. I guess if you hate someone long enough, you become them." An uncomfortable silence develops among us. The four of them stand there without saying a word as if waiting for something to happen.

"What now? I yell. What now?" They remain quiet.

The doctor then nods slowly, motioning to his staff. Ricky eagerly moves in, first trouncing his fist against the palm of his hand, followed by Curtis holding a briefcase and Maurice dragging a black bag. My eyes adjust to the light. I can see the bag more clearly. It's not just any ordinary bag. It's a body bag, precisely like the one used for my father when he died. I will never forget the horrific sight of it. The three of them invade my space. Ricky is standing over me. I look up at his hateful exterior. He clears his throat and spits a glob of phlegm into my eyes. My eyes begin to burn. I use my shoulder to wipe it away.

"Maurice, can you please open the bag and let Mr. Mitchell see the toils of his labor?"

"You think I killed someone? I'm not a murderer!" The doctor walks over to me and squats down. His scar looks more repugnant up close.

"It was you and only you. We found some of your belongings near the body."

"If I were to murder someone and let me iterate, by no means did I kill anyone. Why, in God's name, would I leave my personal belongings near the body? What kind of fool do you take me for?"

"I don't use the term fool to describe my patients. I prefer the term mentally ill. When a patient is sick, their reasoning may be impaired. You may have left your belongings because you felt connected."

"Connected to What?"

"Your victim, or shall I say Alexandria." The four observe my reaction like detectives looking for holes in my reasoning. Sadness dwells inside of me. I refuse to show my weakness. I have to be strong. It's hard to believe she's dead. Alex was ready to change her life and start a new beginning. Why did they have to take her life? I'm not supposed to hate. I believe in God, but all I feel is hatred for them. I want revenge. I want to make them suffer for taking her life.

"You didn't have to kill her. What did she ever do to any of you? You're a licensed physician. How can you kill your patient?" He grabs my throat, digging his nails into my skin.

"I didn't kill her, Mr. Mitchell, you did!" His long fingers squeeze my throat tighter, making it hard for me to breathe.

"I... can't... breathe."

"How fitting, the same way you killed Alexandria by cutting off her oxygen. I won't kill you, not just yet. We have an abundance of things in store for you. We're going to have so much fun together," he removes his fingers around my throat. I gasp for air.

"So, you did beat up on Patricia, but she didn't die. She was able to tell her story to everyone. You tried to fool everyone into attempting suicide and pleading insanity. Now you've added Alexandria to your list of victims."

"I didn't beat up on Patricia. I fell in love with her. She turned on me, but I can't understand why."

"I know the reason why, Mr. Mitchell. It's because you tried to kill her, but she managed to escape."

"I've never put my hands on a woman."

"Oh sure, you can tell us anything. Alexandria is dead. We can't hear her side of the story. The world will know her pain soon. The proper authorities will put you away for such a long time. There's no way out. Maurice, open the body bag," Maurice pulls down the thick silver zipper. I cannot bear to watch. I put my head down to avoid seeing her body.

"Ricky, hold his head up. Make him look," Ricky grabs my head, holding me and forcing me to look. I close my eyes.

"Mr. Mitchell, can you please cooperate? It would be much easier for you if you cooperate."

"I don't have to do anything I don't want to do. I didn't take Alex's life. She was my friend. I will not look at her body; I can't. You cannot force me to look at her," Ricky jerks my neck.

"Curtis, open my briefcase. It seems to me that Mr. Mitchell needs some persuading."

I sneak a look at the briefcase. The briefcase is a smooth brown leather. Curtis seats the briefcase near my feet. He then rolls his thumbs over the silver dials to access the code. After configuring the correct sequence of numbers, the briefcase pops open. Twelve thin pockets the size of dinner utensils hold the stainless steel instruments in place. Each one looks more menacing than the next.

"Mr. Mitchell, these are my babies. I don't leave home without them. I would like you to get acquainted with them. They latch onto people very quickly."

"You're insane, you know that?"

"It takes insanity to become genius."

"You call yourself a genius? What's genius about torturing patients? I think this asylum has made you lose your mind."

"I find that very amusing coming from a pastor who speaks blasphemy. I've always wondered how a man can stand before people and preach false doctrine without guilt."

"I have no guilt because I speak the truth," he scornfully studies me.

"Your words are far from the truth. Everything you've told me is a lie. How can you preach to a congregation and rape and beat up women? My chamber here is justified. I correct the wicked. I kindly persuade them to act in an orderly fashion. My positive reinforcement works. It brings out the best in my patients. I don't bring everyone here, only the ones that refuse to abide by my rules."

"Who corrects you and your warped staff?" Ricky elbows me in the back of my head.

"Doc, can I hit him again?"

"Yeah, doc, let us beat his ass," they chime in together.

"No, no, I have a better plan for him. At first, I thought about using my special tools to break him. Then, an idea just occurred to me. If I let the three of you beat on him, or if I use my special tools to torture him, the blame will point to us all. We don't need the state of CT investigating and shutting down this asylum. My solution is straightforward. I will use Sage. Sage has escaped from his room more times than I can count. He's the perfect alibi. What do you guys think?"

"It's flawless," Maurice says.

"I still want a piece of him. Just let me break something on his body. You promised me, doc. I will feel much better," Ricky begs.

"Just let it go, Rick. Sage will get revenge for all of us."

"Curtis, I can't let it go. He took her away from me. So I must take something of his."

"Maurice, remove Mr. Paul's shackles."

"Are we letting him go, doc?"

"No, Ricky, I'll let you break his arm. Curtis, help Maurice hold him down."

"How can you do this to me? You have to believe me. I haven't touched her. I'm a man of God. Please, I beg you, don't do this!" Maurice and Curtis pin me down, stretching out my right arm. Ricky smiles at me.

"Paul, this is for Alexandria. I loved her, and you came along and took her away from me. How dare you? I hope this hurts like hell," he takes my right arm in both hands, forcing it backward until I hear it snap out of place. The pain is devastating. I yell out in agony. My right arm sags from the socket. I have to hold it in place to reduce the pain. I begin to drift out of consciousness.

"Ricky, slap him hard. We can't have him passing out, not yet," he slaps me so hard I fall over.

"Mr. Mitchell, this is only the beginning of your troubles. Sage makes Hannibal Lecter look like a choir boy. We keep him heavily medicated throughout the day. I don't know if he's had his meds yet. We need him to be as violent as possible. Did you know that Sage had once eaten half of a man's face off? His cannibalism is mind-boggling to me. He loves to gnaw on a person's flesh. When Sage gets a hold of you, there's no escaping. The last time he fled from his room, ten staff members took him down. It's the perfect plan for us not to be implicated. He fled from his room and headed straight for you, which he has done many times before."

"I'm not afraid. Sage is only a man."

"You should be terrified. Sage is more than a man. Quite frankly, calling him a man isn't adequate. We call him a beast."

"I don't care what you call him. He can only destroy my flesh, not my soul. My soul belongs to God." "After he tortures you long enough, you will give him your soul."

CHINA

26

The long drive serves as therapy for Mark. He can clear his head and focus on the good times he and China shared as a couple. He considers calling her, but he also figures surprising her will be the better thing to do. He hasn't seen her in weeks. She will undoubtedly be thrilled. Mark sometimes realizes he can be thick-headed to the point of losing everything. If he has flaws in his character, stubbornness ranks high. Mark's way or highway attitude had turned away others in the past. Even as a child, his older siblings gave him whatever he wanted to stifle the complaints from Mom and Dad. Being the baby boy in the family, he could do no wrong in his parent's eyes. When things didn't go his way, he whined and pouted until they usually gave in to him. His adolescent years were more of the same but with less whining. He constantly challenged his parent's rules. He would push for nine if they told him to go to bed by eight. If his mother prepared one dinner for the entire family, she would make something special for him if he didn't like the meal. His brothers called him a spoiled brat and were careful not to repeat it around their parents.

When Mark became a man, he insisted on having the situation his way and expected the opposite sex to wait on him hand and foot. The attention he received from women usually made it easy for him to get what he desired from them. More effort was required of him when he met China. Mark isn't familiar with being the chaser, clearly affecting his pride standing between them. He understands to make it work with China, he will have to create a change. She is well worth it. Mark presses down on the accelerator. The speedometer reads eighty-five miles per hour. When he reaches China, he plans to confide in her regarding his new intentions. He will help nurse her back to greatness. His eternal support by no means will ever grow weary. The world has forgotten about her. Mark is here to stay. She needs him more than ever before. She had once asked him to move in with her. He kindly declined, stating he wasn't ready. This time around, things will be different.

In a small manner, Mark somewhat admired the rich. How lavishly they lived, and If they wanted an item, it was purchased. Price was of no concern. Past-due bills were unheard of. The rich have money to burn, planned vacations at a day's notice, new cars, and luxurious furniture with plenty of leisure time to enjoy their lives. Nothing was off limits. Many of them lived unrestricted. Suppose they had any problems, their money customarily took care of it. That was the perception of those living on the outside looking in. China's currency cannot free her of her problems. Nearing China's mansion, Mark tries to downplay the constant verbal attacks on his character by shrugging it off as insignificant. At times, it was difficult for him not to think about what the world assumes. The media has the power of persuasion. If the powers that be decide if you're corrupt, they portray you as downright filthy. Mark felt inadequate during these low moments, like a small fish in a big pond. Why had she chosen him? He kept his guard up during the relationship, assuming the end would eventually come. Instead of believing in her trust, he was more occupied with her departure. China had given him a chance, and he betrayed her. He vows to himself that this time around will be different. Mark is so deep in thought that he fails to notice no paparazzi are following him. Generally, the same annoying camera crew follows him everywhere.

Mark doesn't realize it until he approaches China's gate. The absence of media surprises him. Before her diagnosis, reporters and photographers from various news stations would camp in front of her estate. How quickly things can turn, he contemplates.

Mark exits his Jeep Cherokee. He stands in awe at the size of her mansion. Mark visited her mansion plenty of times. Each time he saw it, the measure was astonishing. It reminds him of Camelot. For a brief moment, he pictures knights at the round table discussing their war strategy to protect the king, queen, and country. The mansion looks like a fortress.

Upon entering, guests are given access by a guard sitting inside an impenetrable cemented booth. And if one manages to get past him, five guards are walking the grounds locked and loaded. The guard's name in the booth is Jasper Shaw. Mark and Jasper became friends very quickly. Jasper had a unique air about him that reminded Mark of his father. He often told Mark he was happy China found someone with some real class. "*Just because they are rich in all, don't make them any nicer,*" Jasper reiterated to Mark repeatedly. Mark glances over at the empty cubicle. He inspects the gate. To his dismay, it's already open. He pushes the gate forward and gets back inside his jeep. While cruising down her never-ending driveway, the lack of security presence concerns him. China requires protection. How can this be? If the people pursuing her knew of this, her life would be in grave danger. Mark scans the grounds for intruders. He feels edgy. The luminous moonlight forms shadows from the tall trees on both sides of the driveway. Mark stops abruptly as one of the shadows looks like a person. His heart begins to race. He gets out of his Jeep to examine it further. After scrutiny, it's just another form of a shadow. The night makes the mansion appear somewhat creepy. He opens the door using the spare key China had given to him after their first anniversary.

"China, it's me. Can I come in? He stands in the doorway, awaiting her answer. He waits a few seconds and calls out again. China, it's me. I know I didn't call. Please don't be too upset. I know I haven't been the best boyfriend as of late. I've been selfish, only thinking about my interests. I do love you. I want things to work out for us. You're the best thing that has ever happened to me. I can be difficult at times. I know this. Honey, can we please start over?" He listens for her voice. There isn't a sound. Perhaps he should have called first. He could have saved himself four hours of driving. What a waste of time, he thinks. Yet again, he isn't entirely upset with the drive. The road opened his mind and his heart. Mark considers leaving. China can be anywhere. She's probably with Jason. If she goes to the bathroom, he has toilet paper in hand. Something is conniving about his character, but Mark can't place a finger on it.

Before exiting, he changes his heart and elects to stay awhile. He's traveled too many miles just to turn back around. He chooses to wait and surprise her. Mark has something important to ask her. Something he should have done three years ago when she suggested it. Mark looks around the mansion, which unquestionably looks unkempt and abandoned. He imagines China eliminated her hire when she got rid of Kelly. The place is a disaster. Mark begins to clean up and follows the trail of clothes lying around the house. He walks into the kitchen, covering his nose from the unpleasant smell of garbage. The trash cans are running over. Empty pizza boxes clutter the stove, table, and counters. Spilled sticky beverages coat the floor, and dirty dishes in the sink. It's a complete mess and the very opposite of China's character. Mark washes the dishes, mops the floor, and removes the garbage. He then plops down at the kitchen table. His thoughts revert to a time when he and China were happy together. The two of them would hide and chase after each other inside her mansion, playing enticing games of cat and mouse. The person discovered first had to do whatever the other one commanded. It was a fun time. Mark enjoyed every moment. He missed those times. Mark exits the kitchen table and heads upstairs to check the bedrooms. On special occasions, China held electrifying parties for her circle of friends. Some would crash there instead of driving home intoxicated. China keeps the bedroom doors closed most of the time. Mark opens the doors and peers into each bedroom, looking for anything unusual. The spare rooms are untouched. The primary bedroom door is open, which is uncommon to Mark. She told Mark that closing her door gives the home an aesthetic appeal, displaying her 16th-century door carvings from Africa. When Mark peeks inside the primary bedroom, his heart nearly stops beating. He hurries over to China, placing his finger on her temple for a pulse. Her pulse is steady. However, she is out of it. He turns her over, noticing her bruised face.

"China, can you hear me, honey?" He touches her hand softly. She opens her eyes, attempting to lift her head.

"Stay still, China; you may have a concussion. What happened to you? Did you fall?"

"No, I...was...raped."

After Mark discovers her rape, he insists China seek medical attention. China argues against it, citing it will only make matters worse. She does not want a circus show at the hospital. If the media finds out of her rape, the tabloids will have a field day. In addition, everyone in Greenwich will make it their business to get to the hospital. She begs Mark to bring her to Yale New Haven Hospital instead. It is a longer drive but with less attention. On the way to the hospital, Mark has conflicting emotions concerning her rape. He glances at China sitting in the passenger seat. She looks pretty relaxed for a rape victim. She claimed Jason was drunk, but why did she invite him in? Mark stares at her. He also wants to know the reason she's wearing a see-through nightgown if she said he attacked her. Things aren't adding up.

On the one hand, he feels sad and angered about the rape. How could Jason take advantage of China in her condition? He is lower than dirt, and Mark craves to bury him more profoundly than that.

On the other hand, Mark realizes China and Jason are close. After seven years of being in each other's presence, she swore to him they never had a relationship and no intimacy involved. Still, he saw them whispering and keeping secrets whenever they were together. They laughed together, played together, and remained together.

"Mark, is there something wrong? You haven't said two words to me since you found me on the floor."

"I'm just concerned about you. The rape thing is bothering me."

"Mark, don't worry so much. I'm trying my best to forget. It's not easy. He took advantage of my body. I refuse to let him control my mind."

"Aren't you angry that he raped you? He did as he well pleased with you. Where's your emotion? Where are your tears? China senses the trail of his anger.

"Do you think I just willingly let him rape me without a fight? I cried. I screamed. He wouldn't stop. I even managed to dig my nails into his face. That's when he hit me. I don't remember anything after that. He's a man. I fought as hard as I could," she stopped and stared at him. "I know what's going on. Do you think I warranted his behavior? You've always believed we had a thing for each other. I told you we never had a relationship, and you still don't believe me. How dare you sit there and judge me. How dare you!" She cries.

"I'm not judging you, China. Please, honey, calm down. I'm sorry for upsetting you. I know you're the victim," he redirects his displeasure. "I'm just so upset at the thought of him touching you. He had no right to touch you. I will find him. I will take care of it."

"Mark, you don't know what you're dealing with. He's a slippery person. It will be impossible to catch him. He has friends in high places. He knows the country's FBI agents, CIA agents, and detectives."

"Why are you protecting him?" Mark frowns.

"I'm not protecting him. I'm protecting you."

"You think I'm afraid of this clown? He's going to pay for what he's done to you."

"He has extensive training in martial arts. He's an ex-soldier and can fire a gun with great accuracy. He's been around the world and back in combat. Let the proper channels take care of him."

Mark halfheartedly gives in to China to settle her down. He has no intention of ending his pursuit of Jason. He will find Jason soon enough. When they arrive at Yale New Haven Hospital, China is wearing a baseball cap pulled down to conceal her face. Mark informs the receptionist at the desk not to disclose her identity to anyone except the doctor.

DAVID

27

Keisha foiled David's plan to end his life. Her fear intensified after discovering him on the kitchen floor. She refuses to let any more accidents materialize under her watch. David is her responsibility. She promised herself never to leave him alone again. He tried to convince her otherwise, but she wouldn't listen to any of it. Her intuition alerted her as to the real reason why David was on the kitchen floor. It makes sense, particularly after hearing him rant about death. He was in search of Chuck's handgun. She knew this to be the truth. Keisha pretended not to notice, although it upset her entirely. She is barely coping with Chuck's recent passing. For David to contemplate taking his life makes her a nervous wreck. He didn't know it yet, but the whereabouts of Chuck's gun had changed. Keisha learned of the gun's location many years ago. In that course of time, Chuck and a group of angry men, frustrated with the recent car break-ins, drug deals, and prostitution going on in the neighborhood, formed a night guards committee of six males. Each night, one of the six was assigned to observe the projects for suspicious activity. Their lack of trust in the police motivated them to take back their neighborhood from the thugs who were controlling it. Every committee member carried a registered firearm when they patrolled the projects. On the night Keisha learned of the gun's location, it was Chuck's turn to patrol the vicinity. When he left the apartment to go on duty, he was generally careful to put everything back in its original position. Chuck rushed out of the house that night amid rumors of a drug deal going down. In haste, he unsuccessfully secured the floor tile, which Keisha noticed when she entered the kitchen that evening to prepare supper. She hides in the kitchen closet, awaiting his arrival. When Chuck returns from his night duty, he checks the room to ensure it is empty. He then kneels on the floor, pressing gently on the tile, and removes the gun from his pocket. He returns it to its original hiding place. Keisha peeks through the kitchen closet, fuming. She detests guns. How could Chuck bring this weapon into her home with Nate and David? If Nate and David had access to this weapon, what would happen? She storms out of the closet, startling Chuck.

"What are you doing in the damn closet, woman?" He asks, baffled.

"Why do you have a gun in our kitchen?" She retaliates.

"For my protection," He frowns.

"Protection from what?"

"What do you think, Keisha? Protection from these fools running around this neighborhood doing whatever they want and getting away with it. Somebody has to take a stand."

"And what happens when you go to jail for killing someone?"

"I will not go to jail. I will call it self-defense if it comes to that point. I'm a gun owner, along with my buddies. We're taking back our neighborhood," she stares at Chuck teary-eyed.

"You're just perpetuating the same black-on-black crime these young boys are doing to each other. You're no better than they are."

"Then what are we supposed to do, Keisha? Just lie down and let them do whatever they want to us?"

"Chuck, it's always a better way. Inform the police, and talk to your state representatives. Let the local news know about it. Do it the right way. Let your voice be heard."

"Have you been drinking, Keisha? We don't live in Beverly Hills. We live in the Scrantonville Projects. No one is coming here; they're too afraid," he fires back. Keisha alters her tone.

"Will it hurt to try Chuck? Can you please try for me, honey?"

"Keisha, the guys are depending on me. We've planned this for a long time. We have to take back our community. We will not live in fear anymore," Keisha inches over to him. She understands how strongly he feels about the situation. She takes her hand and gently strokes his face.

"I'll do anything you want tonight if you just listen to me."

"Keisha, I can't. I made a promise to the guys. I'm like the captain. I'm the one that got the group started in the first place. How can I back out now? It took so long to get each of them on the same page. And now that I have convinced them, you want me to pull the plug?"

"I don't want you to quit. I just don't want you carrying a gun, that's all. It's too risky," Chuck looks confused.

"I don't know, honey. It won't settle with the guys."

"Can you try for me? If you try for me, I will do anything you ask."

"Anything?"

"Anything," she answers seductively.

When Keisha spoke to Chuck in her seductive tone, it commonly solved their disagreements. Her soothing talk typically became a precursor to a pleasant night for Chuck. Keisha was so good to him, the perfect woman. She worked wonders in the kitchen and magic in the bedroom; he could never get enough. Her intuition to develop something clever in dire circumstances had been one of her skills. She convinced Chuck to listen, and as always, he agreed. From that point on, he never carried his gun into the neighborhood. He coerced his committee members to do the same. Their position in this matter remained unchanged. The men became angry with Chuck for not sticking to the plan. The committee members sensed that Keisha was in charge of the relationship. She is by far the finest wife in the projects. When Chuck wasn't around, his friends often commented about how hot she looked. The men envied Chuck for having such a beautiful woman.

Chuck's inability to put his foot down was the most displeasing aspect for the members. Keisha made all the decisions, so they decided Keisha and Chuck would have no part in their plans. The men voted Chuck out of the committee, which angered Keisha. After that, Keisha made it her business to make things right. She contacted the wives of the committee members. She convinced the women to start their very own committee. Once the committee was up and running, the women contacted other residents to form a neighborhood block watch. The Scranton ladies pressured their constituents and managed to get a sub-station built right next to the projects. If anything went down in their neighborhood, the ladies were the first to know about it. Keisha's all-out effort helped to improve the community. The residents felt safe. The police made their rounds regularly on foot and knew the committee members personally. Chuck never had to carry his gun again. Keisha persuaded Chuck to put his weapon away and secure it.

Keisha has yet to learn what David is capable of. The funeral is Monday, and she needs David there to pay his respects. She has some last-minute errands to do this morning. Leaving David alone is out of the question. Her skepticism forces her hand. She dreads calling her son but doesn't have anyone else to call. The thought of asking him for a favor gives her grief. He will undoubtedly throw it back in her face when the right time presents itself. Calling him means hearing his constant problems concerning the four children he fathers and the lack of money he has to support them. She must hear him gripe about the leg injury that supposedly happened at work, Burger King. Keisha doesn't want to deal with his mess, but she has no one else to look after David. She takes the blame for her sorry ass son. If only she'd been more demanding when he decided to drop out of school in the tenth grade, his life may have been different. Instead of being more productive, he is flipping burgers at twenty-seven. He lives with his drug-addict girlfriend, who claims she is clean and has turned her life around. To think about it all brings on a migraine headache. After hanging up the phone with Nate, she believes the conversation went well. Her head wasn't throbbing, and he listened and agreed to everything. His good mood is puzzling. He will arrive in fifteen minutes. She goes to check on David.

Nate is beside himself. The news he received from his mother made him smile big. It's the best news he's heard in some time. He sits on the white porcelain, daydreaming like he did as a child after disposing of his waste. After emptying half of the glade air freshener, his thoughts shift to David. The great David Parks is blind, powerless, and searching for a way out of his miserable ordeal. It's a time for celebration. He doesn't have an ounce of pity for David. David destroyed his life and chances of ever showing his mother he could have succeeded. Whatever he tried was never good enough for his mother. Once, Nate surprised her with news of him enlisting in the army to protect his country. Keisha responded negatively to his decision. She didn't believe Nate was adept at making it in the military. For starters, he was terribly out of shape. Nate sat around the house and ate everything in sight. She doubted if he could do ten pushups, and Chuck agreed. They told Nate the army required strength and perseverance. Something he knew nothing about. As with everything else in his life, he was unsuccessful. Nate was unable to make it past the recruiter. He lied about using marijuana and failed the drug test, eventually disqualifying him from ever serving his country and disappointing Keisha and Chuck. He botched many things. The source of his failure came from David. He hates David for his accomplishments.

When David left for college, his mother and Chuck were proud of his endeavors. In Nate's situation, his grades weren't good enough for college. Instead of improving, he dropped out. Keisha constantly pressured him to be more like David. Why did he choose to do nothing with his life? Where were his ambitions? What kind of human being is he? He could never escape his mother's wrath. David made his life seem meaningless. Learning of David's accident on the football field made him joyful. Finally, David has failed in something: an outstanding running back and crowd-pleaser no more. He will never run with a football again. Nate had also attempted to become a football player but lacked speed and agility. The other players named him two left feet that always got in his way and kept him persistently on the ground. Nate saw that Chuck pretended to like him because of his mother. He despised

Chuck for this. Everything out of his mouth pertained to David. The conversations about Nate were adverse. Keisha and Chuck complained about how he wasted his life.

"A lazy momma's boy" is what Chuck interjected, undeniably hurting Nate's feelings. His mother would agree with Chuck, which angered him even more. Today, he will take his revenge. It's David's turn to fail. David will soon join his uncle and never be heard from again. If David wants to leave the earth, Nate has the perfect plan for his parting. When his mother informed him David was looking for Chuck's gun to take his life, he was elated. He doesn't know where his mother has placed the gun. Chuck's gun is old and outdated. Nate figures it probably doesn't fire. He has a nine-millimeter of his own he purchased from a street dealer. He's never fired it. Tonight will be the perfect time to break it in and use it on David. Nate arrives at his mother's apartment at the ideal time. He knocks on the door. Keisha looks through the peephole and can't believe how punctual he is. Nate is never on time for anything. His tardiness describes him best. She glances down at her watch. It's fifteen minutes exactly. What a miracle, she thinks. Keisha opens the door.

"Where's David?" He asks.

"Hold on, mister. You're just going to come through that door asking for David? How about Hi mom, how have you been, or at least a hug? I haven't seen you in a week. Where are your manners?" Keisha says, placing her hands on her hips.

"I'm sorry, ma. I'm just so excited to see David. It's been a while since I've seen him. We have a lot of catching up to do," he hugs her, kissing her on the cheek.

"Nate, please don't ask him about his sight, ok? Talk to him just as you would if he wasn't blind."

"Ma, I wouldn't do that to him. I just want to catch up on some things."

"Nate, you seem different to me."

"What do you mean?"

"To begin with, you're on time, and when I asked you to help me with David, you agreed without a fuss. I remember you hated me mentioning David's name," Nate cracks a weak smile.

"Ma, that was a long time ago. We were both very young. I didn't understand then."

"So, now you understand?" Nate is careful not to overdo it. He turns down his act a tad bit.

"It's David, of course, I understand. I will help him. He's my brother. We grew up together. How can I say no?"

"You seem so different. Have you found a new job?" She hopes so.

"No, I love Burger King. They pay me pretty well, and I love the perks. I get to bring all sorts of goodies home. From French fries, chicken tenders, hamburgers, apple pies, you name it. I don't spend much on groceries, and it's just too expensive. I just buy a little. I can eat off Burger King for a whole month. Angie and I love it. Our favorite is the whopper," Keisha listens in disbelief.

"Nate, eating Burger King all the time isn't good for your health. The food is high in calories. You better be careful. Hypertension and diabetes run in our family. I don't want you dying from a heart attack."

Ma, we are both fine, trust me: Angie's off drugs and rehabilitated. The intervention and detox worked. She's made a full recovery. We're starting to plan our wedding," Keisha is appalled. She wants absolutely nothing to do with Angie. How can he marry this poor white trash? Angie has manipulated him, and Keisha can't say or do anything to change his mind.

"I wish you had done better with your life, like," she cuts her sentence short before she can finish. She decides not to say David's name. Nate is helping her, and she doesn't want him to leave.

"Like wh,o ma?"

"I just don't want you two to struggle. You guys barely make enough money to pay your rent. How can you afford a wedding?"

"Nate isn't listening. Her words of comparison absorb him. It infuriates him. He came here to help her, and the very thing that has kept him away from her comes out of her mouth. He takes a deep breath and then gently exhales, releasing his frustration.

"Angie and I got things covered. Our rent is cheap. She gets a disability for the rest of her life. And the money I make from Burger King is sufficient. We can handle it," Keisha refuses to hear anymore.

"Well, let me take you to David. He will be happy to hear your voice," the two of them walk into the living room.

"David, I have someone here eager to speak with you."

"Who is this eager person?"

"It's me, David."

"Nate, is that you?"

"In the flesh," David attempts to stand up.

"Sit down, David. You don't have to stand up. I will come over to you," Keisha clears her voice to get Nate's attention. She waves her index finger. He makes his way over to David before he can sit back down. He hugs David. David reciprocates by bear-hugging him.

"David, how much can you bench press now?"

"Before the accident, I was lifting about three fifty."

"I can tell, 'cause you squeezing the Hell out of me," David releases him, apologizing.

"I'm sorry, Nate, my bad."

"I'm straight, David, no problem. You are still strong, though, just like when we were kids. You stood up for me so many times. When the bigger kids used to push me around, you always took care of them, nearly beating the living daylights out of them."

"I had to. Nate or Uncle Chuck would've done the same to me. He told me to look after you, and I did. I was used to fighting anyway. When I was sent away to that group home for troubled youth, I learned a lot about survival. I had to protect myself. When I arrived, they tested me, like trying to feel me out. First, they insulted my mixed heritage.

The boys called me every name you can think of. The boys called me Oreo, Zebra, half black, half white, not white enough, and not black enough, and they tried to bully me. When that didn't work, this big kid named Sherman stepped in. He was five years older than me. Everyone was afraid of him. He physically abused so many kids in the facility. Sherman sent a lot of them to the hospital. I saw kids urinate on themselves when he approached them. If Sherman wanted what they had, most of the boys gave it to him without a fuss. He weighed two hundred pounds and towered over all of us at fifteen. He decided to try me. At first, I didn't know what to do. I complained to the detention officers. They told me to deal with it. The officers were useless. The officers loved to see us fight so they could bet on who would win or lose. Back then, I called Uncle Chuck every night complaining. He reassured me he was trying everything he could to get full custody of me. In the meantime, he gave me some sound advice."

"Fight first, ask questions later," Keisha and Nate say in unison.

"He told me to beat the shit out of the bully, and everyone else would fear me instead. He told me bullies usually had big mouths, no heart, all bark, and no bite. He said if I hit him hard enough, he will probably piss in his pants. So, I followed his words of wisdom as I usually did. And it worked. I had no more problems after that. I smashed his face in. His bottom lip needed stitches. I made him give his lunch to me for at least a month. It was payback for terrorizing everyone else."

"That describes your Uncle perfectly. He feared nothing," Keisha covers her mouth, trying to hold back her grief.

"Mom, are you ok."

"Let me be. I need more time to mourn. I'll be back right back. I have to run a few errands. David, is there anything special you need from the store?"

"No, I'm fine."

"Nate, what about you?"

"I'm good."

OK, I'll see you two in a little bit."

With his mother momentarily out of the picture, Nate has the opportunity he needs. The sight of David's handicap and his touching story doesn't diminish the feelings he has for him. It further powers his vengeance. He fixates his vision on David's fair skin, green eyes, and curly hair. Many girls were more interested in David's characteristics and repeatedly ignored Nate. Whenever he invited a female over, and she happened to see David, he was no longer their interest. The girls immediately became concerned with David and asked many questions to learn more about him. One look at David, and they lost control. Subsequently, Nate stopped bringing girls to his home and refused to let David meet any of them. His relationships were kept a secret. When he met Manuela, everything changed. It was love at first sight. The moment he saw her, he knew she was the one. Manuela's parents are from Costa Rica. She is bilingual and has the prettiest face he'd ever seen. Her smile constantly warmed his heart. He did everything and anything for her. He dreamed of having a family and spending the rest of his years with Manuela. After about a year of dating, Manuela pressured him to meet his family. Up until that point, she knew very little about his family. His family was still a mystery to her. Nate decided to go against his premonition and bring her home to meet his family.

After meeting Chuck and his mother, Manuela is thrilled. Keisha and Chuck are also impressed by how bright she is. Manuela is a straight "A" student and plans to attend college to become a doctor. She elaborates on their relationship, telling Keisha they are perfect for each other. Manuela even helped Nate pull up his grades and focus on college. Keisha considers she's a pure blessing.

The evening went very smoothly. Nate felt at ease with how the evening had turned out. On their way outside, David steps through the door. Nate turned immediately to Manuela and watched her expression. David introduced himself, and Manuela shook his hand kindly. They leave, and Nate walks Manuela home. Nate is elated. She never even mentions David. Not a single word about him. She is the right girl. When the two of them reach the doorstep, he wants to make sure. It's almost too good to be true. The handsome David Parks doesn't affect Manuela. She isn't interested. Her happiness lies with Nate.

"Manuela, what do you think about my stepbrother?"

"What do you mean?"

"Let me put it this way: every girl that sees him sort of goes crazy like he's a God. You know what I mean?" Manuela doesn't know what to say. She tries to change the conversation.

"Why are you talking about David? I care about you, ok? We don't have to discuss him," Nate notices the change in her voice. She sounds a little bothered.

"I just wanted to make sure."

"Sure of what?"

"That you don't have feelings for him," she stares at Nate for a long minute.

"I did once, but he dumped me."

The pain of discovering David's relationship with Manuela wounded Nate's heart. She is by far the best thing that has ever happened to him. Nate stops the relationship from continuing. Manuela protested against his parting. She loves Nate, and she is sorry she ever met David. She does everything in her power to convince him to reconsider. Her efforts are in vain. In Nate's mind, she belongs to David. He never speaks to her ever again. The devastation of losing Manuela forced him to drop out of school. He could not bear to see her anymore. His present anger resurfaces. The years of being second to David have damaged his self-esteem. He struggled in every attempt to live up to David's standards, which made him appear as a complete failure to his mother. Why didn't she give him the same encouragement as David?

"David, would you like something to drink?"

"Yeah, sure," Nate walks to the kitchen.

"How about a beer?" Nate yells from the kitchen.

"A beer is fine."

Nate quickly slides the table away from the discolored floor tile. He puts slight pressure against it, like when David stumbled upon the tile when they were children. David came to him first after discovering the gun on the floor. They were both fascinated with their discovery and promised never to tell Chuck or Keisha. Staring into the bottom, he removes the nine-millimeter handgun from the back of his jeans and places it into the space. He secures the tile and slides the table into place. He grabs a beer from the refrigerator and heads for the living room.

"All we have is Budweiser. Is that ok?"

"Any beer will do right about now. I don't have a preference."

"How long are you staying?"

"I should be out of here soon," he hoped.

"Mom told me to keep an eye on you. She doesn't want you to have another accident, but I just remembered I told Angie I would pick up some dessert before going home. I want to get it now before it gets too late. I don't like stopping once I'm near the house," he stares hard at David.

"No problem, Nate. I'll be here. Where the hell can I go? I can't see a thing. Besides, this apartment is my second home. I know where everything is."

"OK, David, I'll see you in a bit."

David closes the front door, locking it. He doesn't have much time. David moves quickly to the kitchen, trying not to bump into anything. He drops to the floor, but this time, he is aware of the table and moves it over. The floor tile pops up with ease. He reaches into the slot, grabbing the gun. It feels different to him. It's an automatic handgun, a step up from the silver-plated revolver. He slides out the clip. The bullets are loaded. He puts the pin back in. Keisha opens the front door. David points the gun to his head.

"Peace at last," he pulls the trigger.

PAUL

28

Janice Johnson has never kept a secret her entire life. As a little girl, she was intrigued by gossip. Mouth all mighty is what most of her friends labeled her. Few trusted Janice to share pertinent information with her. Her mouth seldom stopped moving. Janice insists she has to broadcast essential facts. When a good story comes to her, she rejoices with excitement. Today, Janie has another juicy story to tell, not just one story, but two. She sits at her desk, literally percolating. Everyone around her is busy at work. The waiting area looks like it will never end. As one patient becomes discharged, another one enters. The emergency waiting room is overcrowded with an assortment of ordinary individuals. Nothing in particular stands out amongst them except their injuries. From bleeding wounds to disabled limbs, Janice has seen her sheer of calamities. Janice glances over the patient's contorted faces and painful expressions from their lengthy wait to be seen by a doctor. She pats the top of her black wig several times before the itch dissipates. Chewing her gum like a horse, she glances over the unfortunate. No one draws her attention, unlike the two earlier this morning. The woman in the wheelchair with her hat pulled down to conceal her face could not fool Janice. As soon as the sliding doors had opened, Janice knew it was China Reynolds. She purchased every song China had ever written. She went to many concerts and watched her videos several times. Her chiseled boyfriend looked even better up close.

The tabloids had smeared his name. When he informed Janice to keep things under wraps, she agreed, lying through her teeth. She is not the one to keep a secret. Then, several hours later, another familiar person entered the emergency room, but his arrival came via ambulance. When the paramedics brought him in, Janice asked a coworker to tend to the desk so she could find out more information about the patient. To her surprise, it was David Parks, the great running back from Canada who lost his sight from a severe concussion suffered on the field. She found out he tried to commit suicide, but the bullet missed his brain by inches. The doctors are operating to remove it. Tapping her red fingernails against the desk, she scrolls through her contacts list. The information is boiling over, and she must release it. She looks over her connections and wonders which names would benefit from her exciting news. Halfway through the list, she stops scrolling. Her heart throbs with anticipation. She clicks on her cousin's name—and the phone rings.

"Hello?"

"Girl, it's Janice."

"Janice? I haven't heard from you in decades. Are you still on the planet?"

"Funny," she replies, smacking her gum. I have some news for you. It's something that will raise your spirit and maybe your pay."

"What do you know about my pay? Oh, I almost forgot, you know everything and tell everything."

"If you're still mad at me for telling the family that your boyfriend left you for another man, I apologize. I didn't mean it. It slipped out."

"Janice, nothing slips out of that big mouth of yours. Ever since we were children, you ran your mouth off. It's the main reason people stay away from you. Your gossip hurts. The family keeps things from you because they can't trust you with their secrets."

"You have a lot of nerve to lecture me about gossip. At least my gossip isn't worldwide. Your gossip destroys people's lives."

"It's my job. I get paid to do this."

"So, if I get paid to gossip, will I be more like you?"

"When you take up journalism and learn how to write and report, maybe."

"I have some news I think you will find beneficial. After I tell you, we should be even."

"I doubt that seriously."

"Try me."

"Ok, what hush-hush info are you ready to leak?"

"You have to say the password," Janice laughs.

"Janice, don't play with me. I don't have time to waste. I'm a busy woman."

"I guess it's not that important then."

"Janice, I don't know of any passwords. What are you talking about?"

"Remember when we were children and had a password for entering our rooms?" Danita ponders over it.

"Pizza?"

"Yes, it was our favorite thing to eat."

"So what do you have to tell me?"

Danita Stokes has seen better days working for channel 7Newss. When she first arrived, the stories were plentiful to report. The news reporters worked together to share information with their coworkers to help inform the public from different points of view. The camaraderie changed within a blink of an eye. She is one of three African Americans working in the newsroom but the only woman. Reporting is something Danita takes pride in. She makes sure the facts are all together if she reports a story. Reporting false news is a guaranteed way to lose her job. The fierce competition in the newsroom puts everyone on edge. Good stories are hidden and given to select reporters in today's news era to help boost their careers.

With social media more and more on the rise, reporters are becoming like dinosaurs. As the new wave of young white female anchorwomen parade into the newsroom, finding a good story has become more complex than ever. Their tight-fitted clothing and sought-after young bodies make it problematic for Danita to compete. When a good story comes in, they are usually the first to get their hands on it. Long were the days of being the new girl on the block when the men in the newsroom wanted nothing but her. The men competed for her, placing stories on her desk, and did everything they could to get next to her. Danita has fair skin, intelligent brown eyes, and natural full lips. White men find her easy on the eyes and a sure winner to introduce to Mom and Dad. Sometimes, she wonders if her fair, almost white complexion or hard work makes her so desirable. She's never had a thing for white men. Danita can never forget the history of how her ancestors suffered at the hands of white men.

She realizes racism will never end. The two black men working in the newsroom alongside her are constant reminders. The discrimination the two men receive from their white counterparts is appalling, along with the invisible glass ceiling keeping them from advancing. Danita stares at the plaque on the wall of her home office. The plaque was given to her by the newsroom executives after she successfully reported the story on Pastor Paul Mitchell. Her short documentary on the rise and fall of Paul Mitchell sent shockwaves through the African-American community. Some hated her for denouncing the pastor, while others found her story a guaranteed eye-opener. Her emails included encouraging words as well as death threats. As time passed, the threats decreased as the citizens of New Haven learned more of the truth. It has been long since she had a story of this magnitude and something the masses will devour. Danita senses the walls closing in on her journalism profession at News 7.

Danita's forced to put something together fast or lose her position in the newsroom. As of late, her stories are unimportant compared to the other reporters. She reports stories no one cares to listen to. Her days of producing sizzling, tantalizing news have been few and far between. Janice's information has the possibility of jumpstarting her career. The stories crossing her desk must have accurate information. The source of the story has to be reliable, and whatever comes out of the horse's mouth has to be credible. Janice has both of these attributes. Few agree with her method of spreading dirt, but Danita identifies her information as genuine. She types in her password on her laptop and starts brainstorming her report.

The sorrow she feels for China Reynolds will show in her report. How could her bodyguard rape her in this condition? It's despicable. He deserves severe punishment. Danita's story will help China's departing fans return and support her as they once did before her accident. She will be the first to report the rape of the global icon heard around the world echoing her sentiments. After that point, her report will get even steamier with the news of David Park's unsuccessful suicide attempt. There were rumors of the New York Giants showing interest in his running back skills before he lost his sight. The discussions inside the sports arena talk of nothing else. How unfortunate it is for him to lose his sig from a blow to the head. Headlines continually surface with the need for football helmets to be better insulated to withstand impacts. Concussions have become the league's number one priority. After brainstorming her report, Danita calls her cameraman.

"I have a job for you."

"What job?"

"Meet me at Yale New Haven Hospital in a half hour."

"The Hospital?"

"Yes, Yale."

"I'll be there with the truck loaded."

Bedford Mental Institution:

The disturbance outside the chamber distracts our attention, and the light inside the room has dimmed as an eclipse forms.

I use this opportunity to confiscate one of the tools from the open briefcase near my feet. After grabbing the tool unobserved, I quickly covered myself with the wool blanket. The towering shadow covers the door space. His grunts sound terrifying. Five staff members are holding chains linked to his wrists, ankles, and neck. The staff members struggle to pull him past the doorway. His grunts grow more vociferous. I'm not frightened by the sight of him. He looks like a giant. His face resembles a child. He looks like a boy with smooth ivory skin, sparkling blue eyes, and matted blond hair. It's hard to believe from the sight of his menacing frame and heinous sound that his face can appear so innocent-looking. I wonder what transpired in his life for him to become who he is now. I'm sure he won't give me the chance to find out. A staff member tugs on the chain aggressively around his neck. Sage turns in his direction and heads for him.

"Sage, I have someone here for you today. I know you haven't had too many friends as of late. How would you like to have a playmate today?" His grunting stops. His eyes move from side to side in a rapid rotation. He opens his mouth, but his words barely come out.

"A...fr fr friend?" His deep voice stammers.

"Yes, Sage, a permanent friend. You can play whatever game you want with your new friend. He doesn't mind Sage. He needs a friend also. He's very lonely in here," Sage says, puzzled.

"Why...he...here?" Sage asks, smiling down at me.

"That's an excellent question, Sage. You're so curious," he patronizes him. "Oh, I almost forgot to tell you. He's done something terrible. You know how I feel about wrongdoings?"

"No punishment. I want no punishment. Me no want punishment!" He grunts louder, pulling against the chains. The staff members struggle to hold him back.

"Calm down now. The punishment isn't for you, Sage. It's for your new friend," the doctor says concisely. His theatrics stop.

"What...he...do?" Sage peers down on me, frowning.

"He hurt Alexandria," I brace for his reaction and his antics to escalate, but he manages his composure. His grunts return, and he never takes his eyes off me.

"I punish him for her," he responds.

"I knew you would, Sage. I can always count on you. Men, take Mr. Mitchell's chains off. Ricky, get my briefcase. Mr. Mitchell, have fun. I shall see you soon enough. I don't know what condition you'll be in, but I should return before he kills you. Are you hungry, Sage? He nods to the doctor. Well, his flesh is yours for the taking. Just keep him alive. Do you understand?"

"Me, understand."

When the door closes, the room becomes dark. I stand up, holding my dislocated arm in place while trying to keep the wool blanket from falling off of me. The only advantage I have is the darkness. We cannot see each other, but his grunts reveal his location. I cling against the wall. I move as far away from him as I can. Sage edges in closer. He cuts off the room like a prizefighter in a boxing ring. He's close to me, grunting harder and faster with avid anticipation. He will have me in seconds if I stay against the wall longer. I tighten my hand around the tool in my possession. It feels like a long switchblade. I slide my thumb around the sharp end. It breaks my skin. The warm blood trickles down my finger onto my feet. Sage is standing over me. He reaches down to grab me. I get on my knees. I crawl underneath his legs, slipping away from him. He grabs hold of the blanket instead. Frustrated, he groans harder. My dislocated arm is wincing from balancing myself on the floor. I can't hold myself up much longer. I wrap myself around his leg. He stumbles and then quickly regains his equilibrium. His fists are crushing my back.

He hits me again, and again, and again. His punches descend from every angle. I slide further down his leg to evade his blows. He yanks me by the arm. He tugs it further out of place. I want to die from the pain. I stab the tool into his leg. It fails to slow him down. The stabbing only angers him more. He pounds his fist into my head, dazing me. I pull the tool out of his leg. I'm disoriented. I try my best to concentrate. He stands over me, laughing while enjoying my struggle. He grips my neck with both hands, pulling me off the ground toward his face. He brings me in closer. His repulsive breath is against my cheek. Nausea sets in. He licks my face as if tasting his dinner before taking a bite of me. I raise my good arm in a swift motion, slashing his face from left to right. He throws me on the floor, crying out in pain.

I hear his guided missteps. He whirls around the chamber aimlessly. Again, I latch onto his leg, feeling for his Achilles tendon. I slice both tendons. He squeals and collapses. The floor vibrates from his fall. I stay fixed in my position. My heart is racing. My hands are trembling, covered in his blood. He continues his pursuit and crawls in my direction. I circle the chamber, guiding him near the wall. He follows after me. I wiggle the chains to bring him in closer. He reaches out for me. I take the chain links and snap them around his wrists. He tries to free himself. He yells at me to unchain him. I move backward for my safety. I listen to his struggle. He is unable to break the chains. His grunting slows down. I proceed to go near him.

"Sage, I'm a good man. Do you understand me?"

"You, you, hurt me."

"I know I hurt you, but I had to defend myself. You came after me. I didn't want to hurt you. You gave me no other choice. I'm sorry for hurting you."

"I need a doctor. I hurt bad."

"The doctor will come. Just hold on a little longer."

"Why did you kill Alex?"

"Sage, I didn't kill Alex. I cared about Alex. I'm not a murderer. She was my friend, and I will miss her."

"My friend, too."

"I will find out who killed her."

"Did the doctor kill her?"

"I don't know Sage. I don't know. She didn't deserve to die like this. Sage, do you like games?"

"Yes, me like games."

"Well, maybe if we play a game, it might take your mind off your pain."

"I like that."

"Do you like to play the game pretend?"

"Pretend?"

"The both of us will pretend that we are dead. When the doctor returns, he will be in for a surprise when we jump up and scare him. Does that sound like fun to you?"

"Yes, fun to me."

"Ok, you lay there pretending to be dead, and I will lie underneath the blanket. When the doctor touches us, let's say surprise and scare him. You got it?"

I got it. I like it."

I feel relief. God has spared my life. But now, the state will charge me for the murder of Alexandria. I must find a way out of this. I have feelings for Alexandria. I could never hurt her, let alone kill her. The doctor truly believes I murdered her. I have to escape from this place. Sage unknowingly agrees with my plan. It's not the best plan, but worth saving my life. Before the chamber door reopens, I position myself next to Sage. I use the blanket to wipe the remaining blood off my hands. I keep the tool in my hand, placing the blanket over my body in hopes the doctor will examine me first. As I lie here staring into the darkness, my thoughts regarding Patricia return. How did I let myself fall, and why is she trying to destroy me? I cherished her. She only had to ask, and I would've given her anything. Her deception alarmed me. It left an open wound in my heart. How could she turn on me without warning? There was no legitimate reason for her betrayal. The chamber door opens. I hear oncoming footsteps. I reposition my hand around the tool.

"Sage?" The doctor calls out. "Sage?" He calls out again. "What a bloody mess!" The doctor removes the blanket from me. Sage yells out, "Surprise!" I spring to my feet, grab the doctor around the neck, and place the tool inches from his eyes. The staff moves in.

"Stand down, or I'll cut his eyes out."

"Mr. Mitchell. There's nowhere to go and no way out."

"Quiet, I want you to tell them to remove their clothing and place their transmitters on the floor."

"He can't kill all of us, doc. Let us try to free you."

"Ricky, do as he suggests. He's already sliced up Sage and killed Alexandria."

"He's outnumbered. We can take him."

"I don't want to lose my eyes. Do as Paul says. That's an order!" After the last staff member undresses, I tell them to face the wall. With the doctor in my grasp, I kick every radio transmitter into the hallway. I force the doctor to use his keycard to lock the door.

"What now, Mr. Mitchell? Your options are running out," he laughs. I jerk his neck tighter, drawing the tool closer to his eyes.

"Take off all your clothes," he undresses.

"You will never get away, Mr. Mitchell. Where will you go? This asylum is out in the sticks. There's nothing nearby to help shield you. You will be in the opening for the police to pick you up on sight."

"Hand the clothes to me and get on your knees!"

"When we catch you, you'll wish you were dead."

"Stop talking, and lay down on the floor," I change into his clothes and shoes. The fit isn't my size, but it must do for now. I roll up the pants legs, sleeves, and sports coat to adjust the size. I check every pocket for anything that can assist me in escaping.

"What do we have here, doc?" I shake the keys from his jacket pocket. He doesn't answer. It looks like keys to a Ford. "How about that? You just said I didn't have a way out of here. I thank you kindly for assisting me."

"You'll never make it to my vehicle."

"Not by myself, of course, but with your willing participation."

"I will not help you. You will die in here, Mr. Mitchell," he says with his face against the floor.

"I very much doubt that doctor. If I die, you die. As you said earlier, I've already killed a person, so what's one more but another notch on my belt, right?" I have to play the role of a crazed murderer to keep the doctor off balance. The more he believes, the more he will listen and follow and follow my directions.

"My car is parked near the surveillance cameras. The guard at the front desk will see you and notify the police."

"When we get outside, you will radio the front desk with one of these transmitters informing him not to call the police. If he does, I will kill you."

"He will not fall for it."

"Then, for your sake, you better make it sound convincing."

"You expect me to walk outdoors naked in freezing temperatures?"

"I expect you to do anything I tell you to do if you want to see another day. You have a short-term memory. You stripped me of my clothing in which I nearly froze to death, and you want me to have sympathy for you? Now get up. Let's get moving. You're fortunate to have on your underwear."

In a dash, we walk through the chamber, passing every cell. The doctor leads me to a staircase with a trap door above it. We ascend the latter with the doctor a step ahead of me. Once outside, the numbing cold climate attacks us. The icy weather makes it challenging for the doctor to keep moving. I nudge his back, demanding him to radio the front desk. He makes the radio transmission, pleading with the guard not to call the police. After almost five minutes of arguing back and forth with the guard, the gate in the parking lot opens. Upon reaching his vehicle, I force him inside the trunk. I hear him kicking and screaming as I drive down the open road. I pull over quickly, making a brief stop.

"Doc, hush up before I give you something to scream about. I have to drive this car without any unnecessary attention. If anyone notices me, you will pay with your life," my short conversation silences him. The rest of the ride is smooth sailing. I keep an eye out for police while simultaneously checking the rearview mirror.

I turn off I-95 south and enter the New Haven exit. I ditch the vehicle in front of the New Haven green with the doctor inside the trunk. My house is the first place they will search for me, so I avoid it. I walk past Yale University, eluding eye contact with anyone passing me. I retain an even stride with people walking next to me. I button the doctor's sports jacket to my neck and pull up the collar to stay warm. I stick my hands inside the pockets and keep my head lowered. I need medical attention for my arm. They will probably recognize me if I arrive at the hospital's front desk.

Thanks again for purchasing my second installment of "A Second Chance." The third and final installment is available now! I hope you enjoy it. Happy reading!

Don't miss out!

Visit the website below and you can sign up to receive emails whenever Edmond White publishes a new book. There's no charge and no obligation.

https://books2read.com/r/B-A-DMSDB-RWKWC

Connecting independent readers to independent writers.